HONEY, I BLEW UP THE KID

HONEY, I BLEW UP THE KID

A Novel by Todd Strasser
Based on the Motion Picture from Walt Disney Pictures
Co-Producer Dennis E. Jones
Executive Producers Albert Band and Stuart Gordon
Based on Characters Created by Stuart Gordon & Brian Yuzna
& Ed Naha
Based on the Screenplay by Thom Eberhardt and Peter Elbling
& Garry Goodrow and Story by Garry Goodrow
Produced by Dawn Steel and Edward S. Feldman
Directed by Randal Kleiser

Hippo

Scholastic Children's Books,
Scholastic Publications Ltd.,
7-9 Pratt Street, London NW1 0AE

Scholastic Inc.,
730 Broadway, New York, NY 10003, USA

Scholastic Canada Ltd.,
123 Newkirk Road, Richmond Hill,
Ontario, Canada L4C 3G5

Ashton Scholastic Pty Ltd.,
PO Box 579, Gosford, New South Wales,
Australia

Ashton Scholastic Ltd.,
Private Bag 1, Penrose, Auckland,
New Zealand

First published by Scholastic Inc. 1992
First published in the UK by Scholastic Publications Ltd. 1993

Copyright © 1992 by The Walt Disney Company

ISBN 0 590 55362 3

Printed by Cox & Wyman Ltd, Reading, Berks

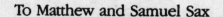
To Matthew and Samuel Sax

HONEY, I
BLEW UP
THE KID

1

A new day was beginning in the Nevada community of Vista Del Mar. The sun had risen a few hours before, revealing a perfect blue Nevada sky marred only by a few dark clouds on the western horizon. Its rays warmed the paved roads that wound through the community of large Mediterranean-style homes with red tiled roofs. Wisps of morning vapor rose from the streets, and the automatic sprinklers that had dampened the small, perfectly manicured lawns in the early morning hours now retreated into their recessed positions beneath the grass.

As the temperature began its daily climb, two women jogged slowly along the street, passing mailboxes on wooden posts near the curb. Each mailbox proudly displayed the name of the home's owners—the Browns, the Carters, the Smiths, the Bakers, and on and on. Like the houses these families lived in, the mailboxes and the names on them reflected a certain comforting sameness.

There was, however, one exception, and as the women jogged toward it, they noticed they were not alone in finding this mailbox out of the ordinary. Ahead of them the mailman, who tried to make his deliveries before the sun got too hot, had stopped in front of the home of Wayne Szalinski and his family. Unlike the other mailboxes on the street, the Szalinskis' had a built-in sensor that detected the presence of body heat, instantly signaled the blue plastic light atop the mailbox to flash and rotate, and caused the door to open automatically.

No sooner did the mailman put the mail inside than the door snapped shut. The mailman shook his head and continued on his morning route. Behind him, the two women, whose names were Janet and Patty, paused in front of the Szalinski house to watch a small white-and-brown shaggy-haired mutt trot down the front path and across the lawn. The dog, whose name was Quark, stopped at the mailbox and pulled a small lever that caused the box to tilt and spill out the mail. Quark picked up the mail in his mouth and trotted back to the house.

Janet and Patty stood in the street and watched the mailbox right itself. The blue light stopped turning.

"I hear Mr. Szalinski is some kind of inventor," Patty said.

Janet stepped closer to the mailbox and studied it closely. "Did the Architectural Committee approve this?"

"Don't get your dander up," Patty said. "Besides,

we've got the kid's party to prepare for this afternoon, and I really don't want to miss 'Family Feud.' "

"I guess you're right," Janet said with a sigh, and the two of them jogged off.

Inside the house, Diane Szalinski stood in the bright, airy kitchen, lost in thought while she waited for the coffee machine to brew a fresh cup of morning coffee. Diane was an attractive woman in her early forties, with freckles and long, thick golden-blond hair. As she gazed out the kitchen window at the desert landscape and the few dark clouds hovering over the mountains in the distance, she couldn't help but feel amazed by the events that had brought her and her family to Nevada.

Several years had passed since her husband, Wayne, had accidentally shrunk their kids Nick and Amy, as well as the Thompson kids from next door, and they'd had that terrible time trying to find their way back home through the backyard. Diane never expected that Wayne's shrinking machine would become such a success after that. She never expected to find herself living in a house like this. As she ran her fingers over the expensive green granite countertop, she couldn't help recalling the cramped, messy little kitchen in their old house at 644 Sycamore back in California. That old gas stove and the ancient dented toaster that always burned the toast, the grimy yellowed counters that never got clean. Of course, her new kitchen wasn't *that* much different from the old one: It, too, was filled with an amazing array of Wayne's strange inventions, all designed to make food preparation and cleanup easier, which Diane doubly appreciated now that they had a baby in the house again.

Adam! Just where was her two-year-old son? Diane turned toward the doorway and called, "Wayne?"

There was no answer. Diane called louder. "Wayne!"

Wayne couldn't hear her because he was upstairs testing one of his newest inventions, the Magi-Shave, which consisted of a large circular mirror held in front of his face by a strap that went around his head. On either side of the mirror were places for shaving cream, a razor, mouthwash, deodorant, and a toothbrush to dangle. Wayne presented a rather odd appearance while using his Magi-Shave, especially because he was wearing only a shirt and boxer shorts.

"Wayne!" Diane called even louder.

Hearing his wife's voice for the first time, Wayne pressed a button, causing two small servomotors to raise and tilt the mirror out of the way.

"Yes, honey?" he called back.

"Where's the baby?" Diane asked.

"In the playpen," Wayne answered.

"He gets out of the playpen," Diane said.

"Not anymore," Wayne said. "I fixed it!"

But just to make sure the playpen was operating correctly, Wayne decided to go into the nursery. As he walked along the hallway, he couldn't help wishing that the rest of his life could give him as much pleasure as his youngest son did.

Wayne entered the nursery. Diane had done a lovely job of decorating the room with white wallpaper covered with a colorful flying kite pattern, but her husband was oblivious to the decorations. His attention was focused on one of his newer inventions—the Auto-Tend Playpen.

Wayne looked into the playpen and smiled. Blond-haired Adam was sitting in the middle of it, apparently quite content as the playpen rocked slowly back and forth. From a speaker at the top of the playpen a synthesized voice said, "See the cat?" and a mechanical cat face appeared on a screen, smiled, and said, "Meow." Little bells jingled and rattles rattled. The synthesized voice said, "Can you say cat?" and once again the cat smiled.

Adam stuck out his tongue and gave the cat a raspberry.

Wayne smiled proudly. His son was a feisty little kid. . . .

Suddenly he heard Diane calling again from below. "You fixed it before and he still got out."

Wayne bristled at the criticism. Normally Diane's comment wouldn't have bothered him, but this morning it just reminded him of all the doubters and critics who were making his life miserable.

"He won't get out this time," he called back downstairs.

Then he turned back to his diapered son and patted him affectionately on the head. "Right, big buddy? Your daddy is certainly capable of fixing a playpen."

Adam looked up and gave his father a toothy little grin. Drool dripped from his chin.

"You don't even want to get out," Wayne observed. "You're only a baby, after all."

Adam just looked up at his father and smiled innocently.

In a bedroom across the hall, Nick Szalinski, now fourteen, and tall and skinny, had just spiked his hair with styling gel and pulled on a black T-shirt and a pair of jeans with ripped knees. He flicked on his CD player and turned up the volume. A rock song boomed out of the speakers. As Nick crossed the room to pick up his electric guitar, he thought about making changes to the walls he'd painted jet black. Perhaps they needed a little more color or maybe a few more posters of rock-and-roll bands.

Nick strapped the guitar over his shoulder and started playing along with the song. What he needed to do, he decided, was become a really flash guitarist. Then no girl in the world would be able to resist him, not even Mandy Park, whom he'd once overheard saying how much she loved rock guitarists.

After a couple of minutes, the tips of Nick's fingers began to hurt, so he paused to rest them. The truth was, Nick really didn't care for the guitar. The only reason he'd gotten it was because of Mandy. The problem was that it would take a lot of time and practice to become good enough to impress her, and once school started next week he probably wouldn't have that much time.

"Nick! Breakfast!" his mother shouted from downstairs.

"Okay," Nick called back, "I'm coming." He unstrapped the guitar and flicked off the amplifier and the CD player. He started to leave the room, then remembered his jeans and hair. His mother would freak if she saw him dressed like that. Besides, as a soda vendor at the Wet 'n Wild Water Park, he was required to wear the park uniform. So Nick pulled off the clothes and got dressed for work. As he stood in front of the mirror, wearing his glasses and combing the spikes out of his hair, he faced the same painful realization he'd had every morning lately—that the older he got, the more he looked like his father. His hair was like his dad's. Some of his mannerisms were the same as his dad's. Even the way his pants always seemed a little too long was just like Wayne's.

Maybe, somewhere down the road, plastic surgery would be a possibility. But for now there was nothing he could do. Nick put the comb down and left the room.

A few minutes later, when Nick entered the kitchen, he noticed that his sister, Amy, now nineteen and a tall, pretty blond, was standing near the refrigerator with her arms crossed and a sulky look on her face. This probably meant she and Diane were having another fight. Nick quietly slumped into a chair at the breakfast table. While he was pouring himself some cereal, Quark trotted over with a mouthful of mail, but Nick knew none of it was for him, so he ignored the dog and started to eat.

Meanwhile, Diane put her hands on her hips and gave her daughter that "I-really-mean-it-this-time" look.

"It's decided, Amy," she said. "I'm going to help you settle in. When the taxi comes to get you, we're both going. Period. End of discussion."

"It's not the end of the discussion!" Amy stamped her foot. "Ever since Nick and I got shrunk by Dad's machine, you've been so overprotective. I mean, face it, Mom, I'm not the only girl who's ever gone away to college!"

They'd been arguing like this for weeks, and Nick was getting pretty tired of it. Suddenly he had an idea. Maybe he could kill two birds with one stone—stop the argument and find the answer to something he'd been wondering about.

"Uh, Mom—" he started to say. But before he could continue, Amy whirled on him.

"Excuse me!" she snapped in her obnoxious big-sister way. Then she turned back to her mother. "And besides, Cal State is just thirty minutes from our old house!"

Diane didn't want to argue a second longer. "Amy!" she said hotly. "Enough for Pete's sake! I'm coming with you!"

Amy could see that there was no way she was

going to win this argument. She folded her arms in disgust and slumped sullenly against the refrigerator. The look on her face said exactly what she was thinking: Parents are idiots.

Nick wasn't so sure he disagreed, but right now he did need his mother's opinion on something. "Hey, Mom, let's say you were a girl."

Diane gave her son a puzzled look. "Okay. I think I can visualize it."

"Well . . .," Nick hesitated. He was about to ask a potentially embarrassing question, and he had to get his nerve up.

"What, Nick?" Amy asked impatiently.

"Would you think I was a nerd?" Nick asked. "Just looking at me, I mean."

Before his mother could answer, his sister rolled her eyes and stepped away from the refrigerator.

"It's a rhetorical question, Mom," Amy said as she left the kitchen. "It doesn't require an answer."

But Diane was curious. "Am I supposed to be any girl in particular?"

Nick shrugged. There was no way he was going to tell her about Mandy. "No. Just . . . a girl I might ask to go to the movies or something."

"Take it from me, kiddo," his mother said with a smile. "You're turning into a very handsome young man. You're going to be just like your father."

Not that! Nick thought despondently, and stared into his soggy cereal. A moment later his father entered the kitchen, still wearing the Magi-Shave, his boxer shorts, and shirt. The servomotors had somehow gotten stuck in the "on" position, causing the mirror to flap up and down continuously in front of his face.

At the arrival of his master, Quark quickly hopped up, eager to deliver the mail. But when he saw the mirror moving up and down on Wayne's head, the little dog was so frightened that he dropped the mail on the floor and shot across the kitchen and out the doggie door, into the yard.

Wayne turned to his wife. "Could you help me adjust the servoregulator?"

Nick watched his half-dressed father struggle with the ridiculous device flipping up and down on his head. His mother's words continued to ring in his ears, "You're going to be just like your father." He tried to imagine how Mandy Park would react to his father. Not well, of that he was sure.

Diane found the switch that deactivated the device. Then she noticed that Nick was staring at Wayne, and she remembered the conversation they were having before Wayne had come in. She thought it might do Nick some good to spend a little more time with his father.

"Wayne, dear," she said. "If you and Nick want to go out by yourselves while I'm away, I've got the name of a new sitter who can watch Adam."

Nick straightened up in his chair. Go out with his father? Be seen in public with Wayne Szalinski? What a totally humiliating thought! Nick jumped up and bolted out of the room.

"What's wrong with him?" Wayne asked as he removed the Magi-Shave.

"I think there might be a girl," Diane said a little wistfully.

"A girl?" Wayne's jaw dropped. "Our Nick?"

"He's growing up, in case you haven't noticed," Diane teased her husband.

With all the commotion downstairs, no one had noticed that Adam had escaped from the Auto-Tend Playpen again. As he waddled down the carpeted hallway looking for something interesting to play with, he saw that the door to his big brother's bedroom was open. Normally he was banned from Nick's room, but there was no one around to stop him. Adam peeked in and saw posters on the walls that wanted to be torn down, all kinds of knobs and buttons just crying out to be pushed, and lots of shiny, fun-looking things that demanded to be played with.

A few moments later, right in the middle of having a really great time, Adam heard a blood-curdling cry of *"I don't believe it!"*

He turned around and saw Nick standing in the doorway. Nick's eyes were bulging, his face was red, and his hands were clenching and unclenching spasmodically. Even at his very young age, Adam could tell this meant his brother was not a happy camper.

"Uh-oh," he said, getting up.

Nick stared around his room in total disbelief. Posters had been ripped from the walls, melted chocolate was dripping from the CD player, and somehow Adam had managed to tighten the strings of Nick's guitar until three of them had snapped!

"This is the worst!" he shouted, and took a step into the room, glaring at his little brother, who added insult to injury by putting Nick's Wet 'n Wild Water Park cap on his head.

"Adam go bye-bye," the toddler said, carefully backing away.

"You'll go bye-bye, all right!" Nick cried. "Straight to the next solar system, you little twerp!"

Nick just wanted to scare the kid, but when Adam held his nose and pointed at him in the universal sign for "you stink," he really lost it. The nerve of that little trout sniffer! He was just about to grab the kid and choke him when Diane pushed open the door.

"Nick!" Diane gasped. "Don't you dare!" She rushed past him and gathered Adam in her arms.

"Jeez, Mom, look what he did!" Nick cried.

His mother surveyed the wreckage and wagged a scolding finger at Adam. "No, no, no!"

"Saw-wee, Mama. Saw-wee." Adam pouted regretfully. He took off Nick's cap and let it drop to the floor.

"I should hope so," Diane said sternly. But Adam

21

looked so cute when he was remorseful that she couldn't help giving him a hug and a kiss as she carried him out of the room.

Nick bent down and retrieved his cap, then surveyed his room. It looked like a disaster area. "I don't believe this! It's in-freaking-credible!"

Amy stuck her head in the doorway. "What happened to your room?"

"Adam destroyed it." Nick shook his head in disgust. "And then Mom came in and gave the little jerk a hug and a kiss."

Amy smiled maliciously. "Now you know what it's like having a creepy little brother."

"Gee, thanks," Nick said sourly.

"Anytime." Amy left. Once again Nick surveyed the room. It was such a wreck he wasn't even sure where to begin. The next thing he knew, his father stuck his head in.

"What happened here?" Wayne asked. He'd finally taken off the Magi-Shave and was straightening his tie as he got ready for work.

"Take a wild guess," Nick replied.

"He didn't . . .," Wayne said.

Nick nodded. "He got out again."

Wayne sighed. "I guess the Auto-Tend Playpen needs a little more work."

Nick stared incredulously at his father. A lot more than the playpen needed work around here.

Back in the kitchen, Diane had calmed Adam down and was trying to feed him some applesauce. Adam ate a little, but he found it was much more fun to take it in his mouth and then squeeze it back out through his lips.

"No, no," Diane said gently as she wiped his face with a soft cloth. "The idea is to eat it, not spit it back out."

Adam, on the other hand, was quite certain the idea was to push it back out, and that is what he continued to do. Diane wiped more applesauce off his chin.

"Top!" Adam picked up the cap from the applesauce jar and showed it to her.

"Want to give it to me?" Diane held her hand out.

"No." Adam shook his head and put the cap in the pocket of his pajamas. Diane didn't bother to argue with him. Like most two year olds, he was very possessive with the things he found and was always putting them in his pockets. She could always retrieve the cap later.

Wayne rushed into the kitchen, pulling on his worn tweed jacket. "I got sidetracked with the Magi-Shave. If I don't hurry I'm going to be late."

"Was Nick's room totaled?" Diane asked.

Wayne nodded and gave Adam's nose an affectionate tweak. "Can't understand how he keeps getting out of the playpen."

"Maybe you ought to put the Auto-Tend idea on the shelf for a while," Diane suggested.

Wayne straightened up. "Look," he said with uncharacteristic irritability, "I said I can fix it. I'm not stupid."

Diane was caught off guard by his reaction. "I never said you were stupid. You're the smartest guy I know."

Wayne realized he'd overreacted and quickly tried to make a joke of it. "That doesn't say much for the guys you know." He bent down and kissed her on the lips.

But Diane knew something wasn't right. "Is there anything wrong at work?"

"Well . . ." There were many things wrong, and Wayne knew she wouldn't believe him if he denied it. But rather than reveal all his problems to her, he decided to tell her about only one. "Expanding matter is turning out to be a bit more difficult than shrinking it."

"But you're happy?" Diane was far more concerned with his state of mind than with expanding matter. "I mean, they're treating you all right?"

Wayne was sometimes stunned by his wife's perceptiveness. She had touched on something he was very uncomfortable talking about. "Yes!" he insisted sharply. "Everything's fine! Why do you ask?"

Diane gave her husband a suspicious look. He was definitely acting strangely. "I just remember how excited you used to get, how you always wanted to share everything with us. Now you never talk about your work."

Wayne knew he'd overreacted again. If only life was as simple as it had been back in the old days, when it was just him and his machine up in the old attic. Still, he didn't want Diane to worry, especially because she was about to leave to take Amy to college. He placed a reassuring hand on her shoulder. "Believe me, everything is okay."

Diane still wasn't sure, but before she could say anything more, Amy rushed into the kitchen. "The taxi's here!"

Fifteen minutes later they had managed to pack the last of Amy's college things into the cab. As Amy and Diane prepared to leave for the airport, Nick came out of the house, followed by Wayne, who carried Adam in his arms. Wayne put the toddler down on the lawn.

"You sure you'll be all right with Adam?" Diane asked.

"Hopefully they'll tire him out at day care," Wayne said, "so when I get home he'll go down for a late nap."

Adam suddenly stood up and bellowed, "No nap!"

"Yes, yes," Diane said gently. "Daddy was only kidding." Then she turned and whispered to her husband, "We don't use the *n* word around two year olds."

Wayne gritted his teeth and nodded. It seemed as if everyone was treating him like an imbecile lately. "Is there anything else?"

Even though Nick was still pretty ticked off at his little brother, he sensed that his parents needed some time alone. "Hey, Adam," he said, pulling a few thick blades of grass out of the lawn, "want to see how I can make grass whistle?"

While Adam rushed eagerly toward his older brother, Diane turned again to her husband.

"His lunch is in the freezer," she said. "And there's a chicken in the refrigerator you can heat up for dinner tonight. Just preheat the oven to three hundred degrees and pop it in for twenty minutes. Also, don't forget that new baby-sitter in case you and Nick want to get out. Her phone number is on the refrigerator door...." She tapped a finger against her forehead. "There was one other thing I wanted to tell you...."

"Don't you think I can handle things around the house?" Wayne asked a bit defensively.

Again, Diane was puzzled by Wayne's reaction. Something was definitely wrong, but she'd have to wait until after she took Amy to college to discuss it with him. She kissed Wayne good-bye.

From where he sat on the front lawn, Nick looked up and saw his parents hugging and kissing. Why did they have to do that in public? Next to him, Adam squeezed his nose, stuck out his tongue, and pointed at his parents.

"Pretty yucky, huh?" Nick whispered.

Adam nodded. Meanwhile, Amy was getting impatient.

"Break it up, you guys," she finally said. Then she gave her father a peck on the cheek. "And don't worry, Dad. Mom will get there, realize there's nothing to do, and turn around and come right back home."

She and Diane started for the taxi, but Amy suddenly turned and rushed back to Wayne, throwing her arms around his neck and giving him a big kiss. Wayne hugged her.

"We're proud of you, sweetheart," he said.

Amy pulled back and stared lovingly into his eyes. "Not half as proud as I am of you, Daddy. I love you . . . and I already miss you."

They smiled at each other. Looking at his daughter going off to college made Wayne forget all his problems. Amy took a step back and glanced at Nick, who seemed embarrassed by the mushiness of kissing and hugging. She just smiled at him. She wasn't going to make him kiss her if he didn't want to.

"You know, Nick," she said, "the thing about creepy little brothers is . . . sometimes they grow up to be pretty all right guys."

The cab driver cleared his throat. "If you ladies want to catch the plane, I think we better get going."

Amy turned to the cab, then realized her mother hadn't followed her. "Hey, Mom, you want to come or not?"

Diane followed but looked back at Wayne one last time. "You're dropping Nick and Adam off on your way to work, aren't you?"

Wayne's jaw dropped as he checked his watch. "That's right! Gosh! The time! I'm gonna be late for work!"

As the Szalinski women got into the cab and sped toward the airport, Wayne scooped Adam off the lawn and rushed toward the house. They both had a big day ahead of them. . . .

Back in the house, Wayne had a challenging time dressing Adam for day care. Every time he turned to the baby's dresser to get another piece of clothing, Adam slipped away and headed in a different direction. The pediatrician had told Wayne and Diane that Adam was a highly active boy, but Wayne sometimes forgot until times like this.

"Please, Adam," Wayne begged as he tried to get a pair of corduroy overalls on the child, "please stop running away each time I turn to get something."

Adam just grinned, then stuck his tongue out and gave Wayne a raspberry. It wasn't often that he got to be alone with his father, and he thought this was great fun.

Meanwhile, Nick waited near the front door, wondering what was taking them so long.

"Hey, Dad, come on," he yelled. "I'm already late for work."

Wayne turned toward the door. "I'll be there in a minute," he shouted. But when he turned back, Adam had vanished.

Oh no, where was he now? Wayne got on his hands and knees and found him under the bed.

"Come out now, Adam!" He grabbed his son by the foot and pulled him out. There simply wasn't enough time to finish dressing him, so Wayne threw Adam's clothes into a plastic bag and ran down the stairs.

Two minutes later they were on the road. Wayne was driving, Adam, not yet dressed, was in the baby seat in the back, and Nick was slumped low in the passenger seat with his Wet 'n Wild Water Park cap pulled down over his eyes. Wayne glanced over at him.

"How can you see anything with the cap pulled that low?" Wayne asked.

"I can't," Nick replied.

"Well, isn't that annoying?" his father asked, puzzled.

"Not half as annoying as being seen in this van by someone I know," Nick replied.

"Why? What's wrong with this van?"

"Oh, nothing," Nick said, "except that it's only slightly weirder looking than a lunar space module."

Actually the gray van was a recent standard model. What made it look unusual were the five circular solar panels on its roof and the three additional semicircular panels on each of its sides, all of them connected to the van's solar power plant by a great deal of looping red, yellow, and white electrical cable.

"It's solar-powered," Wayne tried to explain. "It's an incredibly efficient invention. Not only was it created almost entirely out of recycled parts I found in junkyards, but it consumes absolutely no fossil fuel, which makes it completely nonpolluting."

Suddenly the van began to slow down. Wayne looked out the window and saw that the van and all the cars around it were under one of the large dark cumulonimbus clouds he'd seen over the mountains in the west that morning. While the other cars continued down the road, Wayne had to pull the van off the highway and wait.

"It's also completely useless under clouds," Nick observed.

"No, because then I switch to the alternate power source," Wayne said, defending his invention.

"Then why are we sitting on the side of the road?" Nick asked.

Wayne sighed. "Because I left the batteries in the garage last night to recharge."

"I don't think my boss is gonna understand that I was late for work because I was stuck under a cloud," Nick moped.

They lost another fifteen minutes waiting for the cloud to pass. Finally the sun came out, and with it, the power they needed to proceed. Soon they pulled into the parking lot of the Wet 'n Wild Water Park.

"Thanks for the ride, Dad." Nick yanked open the van's door. "Next time I'll walk. It's faster."

Wayne wasn't offended by his son's remarks. On the whole, Nick was a pretty good kid. The next stop was the Vegas Methodist Day Care Center. Wayne pulled up in front of the tall stone church. When he turned to get Adam out of the car seat, he was shocked. The car seat was empty!

"Omigod!" Wayne gasped. "Adam, where are you?"

He quickly climbed over the seat and started searching for his son. The child was amazing. Even Harry Houdini couldn't have gotten out of that car seat unassisted. Wayne found Adam in the cargo space behind the last seat, playing with the old magnifying-glass helmet Wayne had worn to search for his kids the day he'd accidentally shrunk them.

"I bet you wouldn't try this with your mother," Wayne said, lifting him out of the van.

Wayne carried the child through the yellow day-care center doors to the church basement and into a room where a woman with curly brown hair was playing the guitar and singing to a bunch of small children who were seated in a circle before her. When the woman saw Wayne and Adam she stopped playing.

"Hi," Wayne said, putting Adam down. "I'm Wayne Szalinski, Adam's father. You must be his teacher."

32

"Yes," the woman said. "I'm Ms. Topol."

"Well, it's nice to meet you." Wayne was aware that a dozen small children were staring up at him. "I'd love to stay and chat, but I have a very important lab test to get to." He turned and started back out the door.

Ms. Topol cleared her throat. "Uh, Mr. Szalinski?"

Wayne stopped in the doorway. "Yes?"

"Your son isn't wearing any clothes."

Wayne looked at Adam and realized Ms. Topol was absolutely right. The boy was wearing nothing except a diaper. Even the one sock Wayne had managed to get on him had come off. Then Wayne remembered the plastic bag, which was still in his hand.

"Oh, uh, here they are." Wayne put the bag of clothes on a nearby bookcase and once again turned to leave.

"Uh, Mr. Szalinski!" Ms. Topol called behind him again.

Wayne stopped. "Yes?"

"I am a day-care provider, not a nursemaid," she said. "You may dress Adam and then go."

"I tried to dress him this morning, but he refused to cooperate," Wayne explained. "That's why we were so late."

"That's odd," Ms. Topol replied. "I find Adam to be very cooperative when his mother brings him."

Wayne looked at Adam, who smiled back innocently. He loved his son, but it was difficult to believe that he and Ms. Topol were talking about the same child.

"Under any other circumstances I would do it," Wayne said, "but I really am quite late."

"Then I suggest you hurry, Mr. Szalinski," Adam's teacher replied.

Wayne rolled his eyes and dropped to his knees in front of Adam. Was there any place left in the world where people didn't treat him like a two year old?

"Adam," he whispered as he opened the plastic bag. "Please stand still."

Certain that Adam would make a move as soon as he looked away, Wayne tore as fast as he could through the plastic bag, searching for the boy's shirt. The children in the room giggled as the corduroy overalls, a sock, and a pair of child's white high-top sneakers flew in the air. Wayne found the shirt and looked up, certain Adam would be gone. But his son stood quietly before him.

"All right," Wayne said as he rolled the shirt up around the collar. "Now, please hold still while I try to get this on you."

He started to put the shirt on his son and was amazed that Adam hardly budged except to help get his arms through the sleeves. Adam was equally helpful with the overalls, the socks, and the sneakers.

Ms. Topol smiled. "There, now wasn't that easy, Mr. Szalinski?"

34

Wayne knew it was no use trying to explain. He waved good-bye to Adam. "Bye-bye, Son."

"Bye-bye, Da-da." Adam waved back and went to join the group of children.

Wayne dashed back outside to the van. With a little luck—and no more cumulonimbus clouds— he would be only slightly late for the experiment.

A little while later the van raced through the tall wire fence that surrounded Sterling Laboratories, a large modern scientific facility located in the Nevada desert. Wayne parked in a lot filled with sleek, dark expensive cars. He grabbed his briefcase and raced toward the entrance of the building that housed the company's headquarters. But before he could get to the lab where the test was to be conducted, he was delayed at several checkpoints, where his ID card was carefully inspected by guards.

Meanwhile, in a large laboratory lined with flashing instrument panels and banks of computer consoles, a group of men in white lab coats stood around the Szalinski II, a very large, gleaming, ultramodern version of the original shrinking machine Wayne had built in his attic years before.

A loudspeaker crackled above them: "Szalinski test number one-two-seven-seven, crystal group five."

All eyes in the room turned and focused on one man. In his mid-forties, tall, with carefully groomed dark hair and a cold, calculating look, Dr. Charles

Hendrickson enjoyed being the center of attention ... especially because that idiot Szalinski appeared to be late. He tilted the microphone of his headset up to his lips. "Data recorders to high speed. Time mark."

A large digital clock displaying glowing red numerals began to count seconds backward from sixty. The people in the room pulled dark glasses over their eyes while lab technicians aimed the Szalinski II at a blue crystal cube on a large target pedestal. The machine began to whir, and pencil-thin laser rods that ran the length of the silver barrel began to glow. A pinpoint of bright red light hit the crystal cube. As the digital clock displayed 00:00.0, an intense blue pulse of electromagnetic energy burst from the Szalinski II and surrounded the crystal.

It was over in a microsecond. The entire room was silent as all eyes stared at the blue crystal, waiting, hoping, praying for the desired result. Dr. Hendrickson stepped slowly onto the blue-and-white platform that surrounded the target pedestal. A collective gasp spread around the room as the crystal suddenly pulsed and expanded in size. Dr. Hendrickson stepped to the edge of the circular white steps that led to the pedestal's base and crouched down for a closer look. Again the crystal pulsed and increased in size.

"It's working," a technician whispered.

"Shhh!" Hendrickson put his finger to his lips and sternly hushed the man. Then he turned back to the crystal. By now it was more than twice its original size.

Hendrickson smiled to himself. If this test was the one that finally worked, *he* would get all the credit. Szalinski wouldn't even be able to claim he was in the room when it happened.

On the pedestal, the crystal stopped growing and began to vibrate and slowly melt into a blob. Hendrickson scowled and moved closer. The blue blob shook like gelatin, and the men standing behind Hendrickson began to murmur.

Blam! The blob exploded without warning, splattering Hendrickson's face with blue goo.

Darn it! Hendrickson thought—another flop. As he angrily straightened up and wiped the slop from his face, Wayne finally made it through the last security check and burst into the lab. Hendrickson and the others turned and studied him.

"How nice of you to join us," Hendrickson said, his voice thick with sarcasm.

"Uh, sorry I'm late." Wayne gulped nervously. "There were some largish cumulonimbus clouds blocking the sun. I lost a lot of power...."

The men stared at him with puzzled looks. Wayne took this as a sign to continue. "Well, you see, my van is one hundred percent solar ... and, uh, I had to drop one son off at work and another at day care.... Uh, my wife usually takes him, but..."

The men began glancing at one another. Wayne decided they weren't that interested after all and quickly changed the subject. "So, uh, did I miss anything?"

Hendrickson finished wiping the goo off his face and glared at Wayne with contempt. Then, without answering, he signaled the others to follow him out of the lab. Wayne had no choice but to follow them into the hall.

"We've had some success replicating Szalinski's experiments," Hendrickson told the others who followed him as he strode down the hallway. "But reversing the process—in other words, enlarging matter—has us running up one blind alley after another."

Hendrickson stopped and pointed at a large painting hanging on the wall. It was a portrait of a stern-looking yet handsome silver-haired man.

"Clifford Sterling demands results," Hendrickson said. "The board of directors demands results. The United States government demands results. And as director of this project, I—"

"Uh, excuse me, Dr. Hendrickson," Wayne reluctantly interrupted.

Hendrickson's eyes narrowed with annoyance. "I beg your pardon, Szalinski. As project codirector, I intend to deliver results."

Hendrickson turned and started down the corridor again. And once again Wayne felt the need to get his attention.

"Dr. Hendrickson?"

The scientist continued to walk and answered without turning. "What is it, Szalinski?"

"Well, I've been doing some work of my own on the problem," Wayne began. He wished Hendrickson would slow down. It wasn't easy to talk, walk, and dig through his briefcase for his papers all at the same time.

"Now, Szalinski," Hendrickson replied patronizingly, "when you licensed your device to Sterling Labs, you were promised that the finest minds in the country would be working on it. And, let me assure you, they are."

"Yes, sir," Wayne said as he followed behind, still fumbling with his briefcase. "I know that."

"Good, I'm glad." Hendrickson kept walking.

"It's just that I have some notes." With his head down, Wayne searched through his briefcase as he hurried to keep up. A few feet ahead in the hall someone opened a door. Still running to keep up with Hendrickson, Wayne finally managed to find the notes he'd been looking for. He looked up and . . .

Wham! Wayne slammed into the open door and came to a sudden stop. A shower of papers fluttered to the ground around him, and the sound of Hendrickson's footsteps on the tile floor became distant and faint.

The Wet 'n Wild Water Park was a massive plastic oasis in the middle of the Nevada desert. The sun glinted off the huge rippling water slide that descended into the giant pool. Landlocked surfers on brightly colored boards rode man-made waves onto a beach of sand that had been trucked in from California. Young mothers sat in the shade of palms imported from Mexico and watched their small children play in wading pools. And, of course, as with any water park anywhere, there were teenagers. Hundreds of them in one- and two-piece bathing suits, their tanned bodies glistening with perspiration and suntan lotion.

In the midst of this paradise Nick Szalinski pushed a bright red-and-yellow soda cart with a pitifully small umbrella above it to keep the sun off his head. His park uniform was dark with perspiration and stuck to his skin. Sweat seeped through his Wet 'n Wild cap, darkening the material above the brim. The bottoms of his feet burned from trudging along on the hot pavement, and his nose was filled with the coconut scent of suntan oils.

Nick heard a high-pitched laugh and looked up at the Fun Chute, a blue four-story plastic water chute that twisted and curved and doubled back on itself for several yards before emptying into a pool below. As Nick watched, he heard the laugh again and caught glimpses of a body ricocheting down the chute. A few moments later a pretty girl with long, curly light brown hair, wearing a skimpy red bikini shot out of the bottom of the chute and splashed into the pool.

"Gimme a soda." A red-haired kid wearing a black T-shirt waved a dollar in front of him, but Nick hardly heard the kid as he watched Mandy Park stand up in the pool and shake out her wet hair. Gee, she's pretty, Nick thought wistfully as Barry Lusk and Robbie Fishman, two hunky, bronzed football players from school, helped Mandy out of the pool.

"Hey," the red-haired kid said, "I said I want a soda."

But Nick stood mesmerized as Mandy and the football players walked back toward the stairs leading to the top of the Fun Chute. They were talking and laughing, obviously having a great time. He watched the guys let Mandy start up the stairs first and then follow behind. Everything they did seemed so natural and easy, as if nervousness and self-consciousness were sensations they'd never felt in their lives.

"Yo, soda dude!" The red-haired kid tugged at Nick's uniform. "Gimme one already."

Nick turned and frowned. "That's not the way to ask."

"It is when you're trying to get the attention of a space cadet," the kid replied.

Nick rolled his eyes and gave the kid a soda. He knew one thing for certain: That kid would never call Barry Lusk or Robbie Fishman a space cadet.

It was a long hard day, pushing the soda cart around the park under the hot summer sun. As always, it was a day filled with little kids who didn't know how to count change, mothers who complained the sodas weren't cold enough, and troublemakers who tried to reach into the cart and steal cans when Nick wasn't looking.

But the most frustrating part of the day for Nick was watching the kids his age having fun while he had to slave away. It wasn't like working that summer had been his decision. Getting a summer job had been his father's idea. According to Wayne Szalinski, working during the summer had something to do with building character. Nick didn't know exactly what that meant, but he hadn't been left with a choice.

Nick's shift ended at four in the afternoon. By

that time people were starting to leave the park, and Nick fell in with the crowd moving toward the exits. Once again he heard Mandy's laugh. Glancing behind him, he saw that she was now wearing a yellow sun dress and was walking with Barry and Robbie.

Nick felt his insides stir. Tomorrow was his day off and the last Saturday of summer before school started. He had nothing planned. If only he could get up the nerve to talk to her, he thought. If only he could ask if she wanted to do something tomorrow. But just the thought of her made his pulse race and his chest feel tight. This is so dumb, he thought. She's just another human being. It's not like she's some kind of goddess.

As they reached the parking lot, Nick took a deep breath and worked up his nerve. He'd wanted to speak to Mandy ever since he'd first seen her, but somehow he'd always chickened out. It killed him to think about the opportunities he'd passed up. Like the time she'd wanted to buy a soda but discovered she was a nickel short. Of course, he let her have it anyway, but at least he could have said something. And then there was the time he'd overheard her talking with her girlfriends about babysitting for a little kid who was in Adam's room at the day-care center. He could have said something then, too, but as usual, he didn't.

Well, this time he was going to make his presence known. He waited until Mandy and the guys stopped next to Barry's jeep. The guys were talking about something, and for a moment Mandy just gazed around, obviously not part of the conversation. Nick knew this was his chance.

"Uh, Mandy?" he said.

Mandy turned and looked at him. So did Barry and Robbie. In his chest Nick could feel his heart pounding like a jackhammer.

"Yeah, Rick?" Mandy said.

"It's Nick," Nick said.

Mandy nodded. "Yeah, Nick?"

Nick started to open his mouth, but before he could get the words out, Barry Lusk pointed at something. "Hey, look at that!"

Nick turned to see what they were staring at. Across the parking lot, the solar-powered van pulled in the entrance and rolled toward them.

"Is that the strangest thing you ever saw?" Barry said.

"Looks like it was put together from a junk heap," Robbie replied, laughing.

Nick's whole face began to burn. He started to duck down between two parked cars, but it was too late.

"Hey, Nick!" his father shouted. Nick saw his father waving at him through the open window of the van. "Want a ride home?"

"Yoo-hoo, Nick," Robbie Fishman said with a smirk. "Your ride's here."

Nick had no choice but to slink toward the van and get in. As he slammed the door, he looked back at Mandy and the guys. They were pointing in his direction and laughing.

Nick slumped into his seat and pulled his cap low over his eyes. "Nice going, Dad."

"What?" Wayne asked, oblivious to the embarrassment he'd just caused. "What'd I do?"

"Forget it, Dad," Nick said with a sigh. "Let's just go."

They pulled onto the road toward Vista Del Mar. Wayne had picked up Adam at the day-care center before picking up Nick, and for once the child was content to sit in the car seat and play with a toy car.

"Zoom! Zoom!" he said happily as he made it race around.

Nick sat in the passenger seat, replaying in his mind the scene that had just occurred in the parking lot of the water park. It wasn't really his father's fault; he'd just tried to be helpful, that's all. Anyway, Nick figured he couldn't have dropped much in Mandy's estimation, since he'd never had any stature there to begin with. Maybe something good had come of it—she knew his name now... if she remembered it.

Nick turned and studied his father, who tended to lean forward against the steering wheel when he drove, as if it helped him see the road better. His father was weird, but he was still the only father Nick had. There were certain questions Nick couldn't ask anyone else.

"Dad?" he began. "Were you ever very... uh ... popular in school?"

Without taking his eyes off the road, Wayne nodded. "Oh, sure. I was vice president of the Astronomy Club two years in a row. I was a happening guy. Uh, why do you ask?"

Nick stared at his father in disbelief. Could anyone really be that far out of it? Still, there was something that really puzzled him.

"I was curious," he said. "Because Mom was a cheerleader and ... well, I was just wondering how you two ..." He didn't know how to complete the sentence without insulting his father.

"How we two what?" Wayne asked.

"Well, got together," Nick said.

Wayne thought for a moment. "I usually borrowed your grandfather's car and picked her up. Although sometimes Dad and Mom were also going out, so we'd double date."

Nick stared at him. Double date with your own parents? That was the most bizarre thing he'd ever heard.

"That's not what I meant, Dad," he said. "I meant, how'd you two ever get together in the first place?"

Wayne glanced at his son in surprise. "You make it sound like it was a rather unlikely event."

"It wasn't?" Nick asked.

His father was quiet for a second and then said, "It just so happens that your mother is one of those people who is more interested in what someone is like on the inside. Know what I mean?"

"Oh, yeah, sure." Nick gave up. What did it matter what he was like on the inside? He couldn't even get Mandy to look at the outside!

"So . . .," his father cleared his throat. "Mom tells me . . . I mean, is there some girl you're—"

"What?" Nick was surprised and somewhat embarrassed. "Oh, no. I was just . . . you know . . . wondering. That's all."

The last thing he needed was his father wondering if he was interested in a girl.

Later, as the bright summer sun began to drop toward the mountains in the western horizon, all seemed well at the Szalinski house. Wayne had preheated the oven as per his recollection of Diane's instructions and put the chicken inside. Now he sat at the kitchen table, surrounded by his papers, puzzling over the enlargement problem they were having at the lab with the Szalinski II. He knew there had to be a solution. He'd always found solutions to problems in the past, even solutions to stubborn problems, such as Adam's repeated escapes from the Auto-Tend Playpen. At least that wouldn't be a problem anymore. About an hour ago, after bringing Adam home from day care and Nick back from the water park, he had finally made the playpen absolutely escape-proof.

But the problem with the Szalinski II was more complicated than fixing a playpen. It was two problems really. The first problem was with the machine itself and why it couldn't enlarge objects as easily as it shrank them. And then there was the problem of Dr. Hendrickson, who seemed, for some completely inexplicable reason, to have taken a distinct dislike to Wayne. Normally Wayne would not have paid much attention to the latter problem, but unfortunately Dr. Hendrickson was the codirector of the project, and he was making it very difficult for Wayne to get his ideas heard.

As Wayne puzzled over his predicament his eyes began to water, and he grew short of breath. This was odd, he thought. He rarely became so emotional about such things.

Upstairs, Adam was also pondering a problem—how to break out of the Auto-Tend Playpen now that his father had reinforced it. After studying the situation for a few minutes, Adam smiled. He had found a way.

Down the hall, yet another member of the Szalinski family was deep in thought. More precisely, Nick was trying to figure out how he could not only get Mandy Park's attention but convince her that he was worthy of keeping it. He'd pretty much given up on teaching himself to be a great guitarist because it would probably take so long that Mandy would be married and have kids by the time he accomplished it.

Then again, maybe he could learn just a few songs well enough to impress her. But what songs would they be? As Nick considered the possibilities, he noticed the smell of smoke in his room. Uh-oh, something was wrong! He jumped up and ran into the hallway. The smoke was thicker there, and it seemed to be coming from downstairs.

Down in the kitchen, Wayne was practically in tears. Get a hold of yourself, he thought. You've faced serious problems before and found a way to solve them, and you'll do it this time, too.

"Dad!"

Wayne heard Nick's shout and turned around. To his amazement the kitchen was filled with smoke. No wonder his eyes were tearing!

Thick gray smoke was pouring out of the oven.

"Dad, what's in there?" Nick crouched down in front of the oven.

"Just the chicken," Wayne said.

"At what temperature?"

"Uh, six hundred, just like your mother said."

Nick peered through the oven window. Inside something shaped like a chicken was glowing red.

"I don't think Mom said six hundred, Dad."

"Maybe you're right," Wayne said.

Nick began to reach for the oven door.

"Don't!" Wayne shouted. "You'll get a backdraft!"

"A what?" Nick scowled.

"Superheated gases in the absence of oxygen," Wayne quickly explained. "Open that door and you'll create a huge ball of fire."

"So what do we do?" Nick gasped.

"Get the fire extinguisher!"

"Where?"

"In the basement!"

No sooner did Nick dash out of the kitchen than

the phone rang. Wayne debated whether to answer it or attend to the emergency at hand. It could be important news from the lab, he thought, so he picked it up. "Hello?"

"Hi!" It was Diane.

"Oh, hi, honey," Wayne said, trying to sound calm while he fanned away the smoke that was now billowing out of the oven. He didn't dare tell his wife how out of control things were at home. It would just prove that he couldn't handle things without her. "How was your flight?"

While Diane filled Wayne in on the trip, Nick rushed back into the kitchen carrying a large red fire extinguisher.

"So how are things there?" Diane asked.

"Here?" Wayne gulped. "Everything's great. . . . Uh, could you hold a second?"

He quickly put the phone down and picked up a pot holder. "Ready?" he asked his son.

Nick nodded nervously and aimed the fire extinguisher at the oven.

"Okay." Wayne reached for the door. "One, two, three . . . go!"

He yanked open the oven door and jumped back. A huge ball of red and orange flame leapt out of the oven, and Nick sprayed it with the fire extinguisher. The fire hissed loudly. Meanwhile, Wayne picked up the phone again.

"What's that hissing sound?" Diane asked.

"Hissing sound?" Wayne swallowed. "Oh, uh, water. The water's running in the sink."

"Oh, okay." Diane seemed placated. "And how's the baby?"

"Adam?" Wayne said. "Oh, he's just having a fine time in the playpen."

"Are you sure he can't get out?" Diane asked.

"Absolutely," Wayne assured her. "I just fixed it. This time he'll never get out."

But even as the words were leaving Wayne's lips, Adam was indeed crawling out of the playpen. A moment later he bumped his way down the stairs on his behind, one step at a time. At the bottom of the steps, he stood up, trying to decide which way to go. Suddenly he heard the ringing sound of ice-cream-truck music coming from outside.

"I-cweem!" Adam looked up at the front door. The doorknob was out of reach. If only he had something to stand on. In the living room, Adam saw the perfect thing: a small stool his father rested his feet on while he read at night. He toddled over and started to pull it back toward the door.

Quark heard a scraping sound and looked up to see Adam dragging the footstool over to the front door. Sensing danger, the dog jumped up and went to look for help.

In the kitchen, Nick had put on a diving mask to keep the smoke out of his eyes while he probed the blackened interior of the oven with a pair of long tongs, searching for the remains of the chicken. Wayne was still on the phone with Diane, pretending all was well.

"So how's Amy's dorm?" he asked. As Diane

started to fill him in, Quark raced into the kitchen and started tugging at the leg of his master's pants. Wayne swatted at the dog with his free hand. "Stop it!"

"What?" Diane asked.

"Oh, uh, nothing," Wayne said. The only way to stop Quark was to pick him up, which Wayne did. "It's just the dog. So you were saying about Amy's dorm room?"

"Right," Diane said. "It's a little cramped, but her roommate is very sweet. She's from Fresno, and she brought Amy a large basket of fruit."

"How nice," Wayne said, holding the phone with one hand while he tried to restrain the squirming dog with the other. From the living room he heard a creaking sound, as if someone had opened the front door.

"And they've already decided to try out for the swimming team together," Diane was saying.

"That's great." Still holding the dog and the phone, Wayne dashed out of the kitchen and into the living room. The front door was wide open. Outside, an ice-cream truck with a huge, brown plastic ice-cream bar on its roof was rolling slowly up the street. Wayne couldn't understand how the front door got opened until he spotted Adam waddling down the driveway. In a few seconds he'd be in the street!

Wayne dropped the phone and the dog and ran out the door. He managed to grab his son just inches from the curb.

"I-cweem! I-cweem!" Adam cried, reaching with outstretched arms toward the passing ice-cream truck as Wayne hurried back into the house and picked up the phone from the floor.

"Hello?" Diane said.

"Yes, honey?" Wayne tried to sound as natural as possible under the circumstances.

"Funny," Diane said, "for a second I thought you weren't there."

"Oh, no." Wayne forced a laugh as he put Adam down and hurried back into the kitchen. "I haven't missed a word."

"Did you remember to heat up the chicken?" she asked.

As Wayne entered the kitchen, Nick was extracting the charred and smoldering remains of the chicken from the stove.

"I sure did, honey," Wayne said wearily. "And let me tell you, it looks mighty good."

At dinner that evening Quark, who never turned down a table scrap, wouldn't go near the burned chicken, which now rested in his food bowl. At the kitchen table the men of the Szalinski family ate peanut-butter-and-jelly sandwiches off paper plates.

Nick took a bite of his sandwich and pushed the plate away. One look at Adam and he completely lost his appetite. The little kid's face, hands, and arms were covered with peanut butter. Besides, Nick was really bummed. It looked like another day off was going to come and go. In fact, it looked as if the entire summer had come and gone. At this rate he'd probably wind up graduating high school without ever having had a date.

Adam pushed Nick's unfinished sandwich back toward him. "Eat, Nick-Nick, eat."

"You eat." Nick pushed the plate and his little brother's hand away.

Across the table, Wayne had just wolfed down his

second sandwich. Even after he wiped his mouth with his napkin, he somehow managed to miss a large glob of peanut butter on his chin. Nick stared at his father and then at his little brother. Both had peanut butter on their face. Maybe it's in the genes, he thought gloomily. Maybe I've been doomed from birth.

Wayne chose that moment to speak to his son. "You know, Nick, I've been thinking about that conversation we had in the van this afternoon."

Nick stared fearfully back at his father. Although he had wanted to discuss it that afternoon, now it was the last thing in the world he wanted to talk about. . . . It would just reinforce how hopeless it all was.

"Now that the women are out of the house," his father continued, "I thought us guys could have a little talk about the birds and the bees."

Nick couldn't believe his ears. No one had called it the birds and the bees since the invention of sex ed. Meanwhile, across the table, Adam picked up a gooey glob of peanut butter and smooshed it between his hands.

"I thought we'd start with the birds," Wayne said.

"Birds, birds!" Adam gleefully clapped his hands. A glob of peanut butter hit Nick in the forehead just over his left eye.

Nick pushed his chair back and stood up. "I'm sorry, Dad. I just can't take this right now." He was glad to get out of the kitchen.

* * *

Wayne Szalinski never appreciated his wife more than when she wasn't there. No one was better at dealing with petulant teenagers and a rambunctious toddler while still managing to keep a sense of humor. With his shirt front and sleeves soaked with warm bathwater, Wayne carried a freshly washed Adam back into his room and placed him on the changing table.

"Please, just sit still for two seconds," Wayne begged as he searched the drawers for a diaper and clean pajamas. He found both and was amazed to find that Adam hadn't moved. Wayne quickly dressed him and placed him in his crib.

"Big Bunny," Adam said.

"Okay. Here's Big Bunny." Wayne reached for the large tan-and-white stuffed bunny with the green, red, and yellow checked bow tie. Working its arms like a puppet's, he leaned it over the rail of the crib.

"Hi, Adam," Wayne said in a high, animated voice. "It's me, Big Bunny."

The grin on Adam's face was worth a million dollars.

"Did Adam have a good day today?" Big Bunny asked.

Adam nodded.

"Did Adam have fun at day care?" Big Bunny asked.

Again Adam nodded.

"Is Adam going to go outside all by himself again?" Big Bunny asked.

Adam thought for a moment and then decided it was politic to shake his head.

"That's a good boy," Big Bunny said. Wayne thought for a moment and then added, "Would Adam do Big Bunny a big big favor? Would Adam lighten up on his big brother, Nick? Adam shouldn't forget that Nick's been uprooted and moved and it's real tough on him."

Adam stuck his thumb in his mouth and rubbed his eyes, then reached up and took Big Bunny from Wayne. As the little boy snuggled with the toy, Wayne began to sing "Alouette" just as he did every night to get Adam to sleep.

As Wayne worked his way through the verses, Adam's eyes began to close, and Wayne focused on a blue balloon tied to a corner of the crib. It jogged something in his mind, something that had to do with the problems at the lab. . . . Wayne reached over the crib, took the balloon in his hand, and studied it. He could feel an idea percolating in his consciousness. Suddenly it sprang forth. Of course! Wayne snapped his fingers. That had to be it!

Wayne wasn't the only person having a brainstorm at that moment. Back at Sterling Laboratories—now shrouded in darkness except for the lights from the security towers and the flashlights of the security men who patrolled the grounds—other minds were also hard at work. In the lab that had been so crowded with scientists and technicians earlier in the day, two men now stood in the shadows beside the Szalinski II.

Dr. Charles Hendrickson rubbed his chin in thought and then looked at the well-dressed man with slicked-back hair who stood beside him. "So, what do you think?"

Terence Wheeler drained the last drops from a bottle of soda and placed it firmly on a nearby desk. He turned back to Hendrickson and spoke solemnly. "It'll be a hell of a thing for you, Charles . . . if it works."

"It'll work," Hendrickson said confidently. "I'll make it work."

Wheeler looked up at the huge machine that dominated the center of the lab. "Over the years, I've seen Clifford Sterling attach himself to one harebrained idea after another. I have to tell you, Charles, the board of directors is very worried."

Before Hendrickson could reply, a telephone at the other end of the laboratory lit up and rang. "Pardon me," Hendrickson said as he walked across the lab to the phone. He picked it up. "Hendrickson here."

On the other end of the line, Wayne stuck a needle into the balloon with a *bang!*

Hendrickson yanked the phone from his ear. "What the devil was that?"

"A balloon popping," Wayne explained. "I got this idea while singing my kid to sleep. See, if you hit a balloon with too much force, you don't allow the molecules enough time to expand. So the balloon pops."

Hendrickson smirked. "Thank you for the lesson in elementary physics, Szalinski. I hadn't realized I was in need of remediation."

As Wayne began to explain how the popping balloon related to the problems they were having with the Szalinski II, Wheeler joined Hendrickson.

"Is there a problem?" Wheeler whispered.

"Not at all." Hendrickson brought the phone down from his ear and cupped his hand over the mouthpiece so Wayne wouldn't hear him. "It's just Szalinski."

"Oh, him," Wheeler said with a smirk.

"Why Clifford insists on keeping Szalinski involved in this project is absolutely beyond me," Hendrickson said in a low voice while Wayne rambled on. "We'd be knee-deep in apples the size of sedans by now if I were running this thing alone."

"There are those of us on the board of directors who would agree with you," Wheeler said with a grave nod.

Out of curiosity, Hendrickson brought the phone back to his ear and listened for a moment more as Wayne rambled on about something involving a lower intensity of electromagnetic pulse being needed to give the molecules time to expand without tearing the atomic fabric. It sounded like the man's usual gibberish, and Hendrickson once again cupped his hand over the receiver.

"Clifford Sterling may have outlived his usefulness to the corporation and the stockholders," Wheeler said. "I think his successor would be a foregone conclusion." He paused and pointed at the Szalinski II. "Especially if he was the person who actually made this thing work."

As the implication of Wheeler's words sank in, Hendrickson smiled. The presidency of Sterling Labs was at his fingertips. All he had to do was get the Szalinski II to work. The two men shook hands, and Wheeler turned and walked out of the lab. It took Hendrickson several moments to remember that Szalinski was still jabbering away on the phone.

"Hello? Hello?" Wayne was saying. "Dr. Hendrickson? Are you still there?"

Hendrickson lifted the phone back to his ear. "Of course, Szalinski," he said smugly. "Haven't missed a word. Tell you what. Why don't you write up this balloon research and show it to me."

"I could probably have it on your desk by tomorrow afternoon," Wayne said eagerly.

"That won't be necessary," Hendrickson said. "No need to rush it. Have a good weekend, Szalinski."

"But—" Before Wayne could continue, he heard a click as Hendrickson hung up. "Have a good weekend, Szalinski," he muttered to himself, shaking his head in disgust. Hendrickson had given him the brush-off again. Wayne hung up the phone and sat back in his chair, wondering if things would ever change.

Upstairs in his bedroom, Nick sat on his bed, also

wondering if his life would ever change. He turned and stared at the phone, painfully aware that he was facing the last weekend of summer with nothing to do. Then school would start, and everywhere Mandy Park went she'd be surrounded by an impenetrable wall of friends. This just might be his last chance to salvage a summer that otherwise appeared to be a total waste.

Nick took a deep breath and reached for the phone. He was so nervous it took him four tries before he finally dialed the right number. For a second he caught himself hoping the line would be busy, but no such luck. He heard the phone ring.

"Hello?" an older man answered. Nick figured it was Mr. Park.

"Uh, hi," Nick stammered. "May I speak to Mandy, please?"

"Just a minute," the man said. Nick heard the phone click as it was placed on some hard surface. Then he heard, "Mandy, phone for you."

The seconds passed slowly as Nick rehearsed in his head what he planned to say. Soon he heard the sound of hurried footsteps growing louder as they approached the phone. A moment later he heard a breathless "Hello?"

Adrenaline raced through Nick like an electric shock. "Oh, uh, hi, Mandy. Listen, this is—"

There was a click and the line went dead before Nick could get the words out. He lowered the phone and stared at it in horror as if his worst nightmare had just come true. Was it possible that she recognized his voice from that afternoon and hung up on him?

Nick heard a sound and turned around. There, standing in the open doorway of his room, was Adam in his pajamas. And in his pudgy little hand was the unplugged phone line. Nick stared at his little brother in utter incredulity. So it was a nightmare, but not the one he expected. Nick felt his blood begin to boil.

"Why you little . . ." He jumped up.

Adam could see that his big brother was really upset. It was time to beat a hasty retreat. He turned and ran into the hall as fast as his two-year-old feet would carry him, right into the arms of his father.

"Hey, what are you doing up?" Wayne asked, scooping his son into his arms.

A split second later Nick came charging out of his room and skidded to a halt in front of them both.

"Oh," Wayne said to Adam with a smile. "So you were visiting your big brother. Decided to make up, did you?"

Adam nodded very solemnly. Nick glared at him, wishing he could rip the little worm's head off.

"Well, it's time you went to bed for good, little guy," Wayne said affectionately. He started to turn away but then stopped and turned back to his older son. "Hey, Nick, how would you like to help me with something tomorrow?"

"What? Oh, okay, I guess," Nick muttered.

"Sure I won't be taking you away from anything?" Wayne asked.

"Yeah," Nick said, still glaring at Adam. "As of a couple of seconds ago, I've got nothing better to do."

"Great," Wayne said. "See you in the morning."

Wayne turned and took Adam back to his room. Wayne was feeling better: He had finally decided to take action on his own.

It was still dark when Nick felt a hand gently shake his shoulder. He woke and looked up through the dark at his father's face. "Wha . . . what is it, Dad?"

"Time to get up," Wayne said.

"Why? Is something wrong?"

"You said you'd help me, remember?"

Nick yawned, rolled over, and closed his eyes again. "Yeah, Dad, tomorrow."

Wayne shook his son's shoulder again. "It is tomorrow."

"What are you talking about, Dad?" Nick asked, rolling back to face him. "It's the middle of the night."

"Early morning, actually," Wayne said. "The sun will be up in a little while. Now come on, we've got things to do. I'll get Adam up."

Ten minutes later, as Nick dragged his tired body into the brightly lit kitchen, he found that his father had already put out a bowl of cereal for him. Adam was sitting in his high chair, and Big Bunny was seated next to him at the kitchen table. Somehow Adam, dressed in a yellow turtleneck and a pair of red corduroy overalls with a large pocket in the front, was finding it easy to be cheerful at this ungodly hour of the morning. He gave Nick a big smile as his father tried to get some cereal into him, too.

"I don't see what there is to smile about," Nick groaned as he slid into his seat at the breakfast table.

"Now come on, Nick," Wayne said. "You've been up this early before."

"Never by choice," Nick mumbled, adding milk to the cereal. "What's the big deal, anyway?"

"Nothing, really," Wayne replied. "I just need a little help down at the lab."

"Why can't it wait until later in the day?" Nick asked.

"Oh, it's just one of those things that's better taken care of early than late," his father replied with uncharacteristic vagueness.

Nick shrugged. "I don't get it. You never asked me to help you at the lab before."

Wayne gazed steadily back at him. "Believe me, Nick, if I didn't need your help, I wouldn't have asked."

By the time they got out to the van, the red morning sun had just started to peek up over the mountains to the east.

"Did you remember to put the batteries back in?" Nick asked as his father strapped Adam into the car seat. Adam pulled Big Bunny onto his lap.

"Yup." Wayne and Nick climbed into the front. By now the sun was halfway over the mountain range. Wayne pressed the button that unfolded the solar panels, and they were off.

Ten minutes later they passed through the double rows of tall chain-link fencing surrounding Sterling Laboratories and parked. As Nick got out he realized theirs was the only car in the lot.

"Isn't anyone else coming to work today?" he asked as Wayne unfolded Adam's stroller and strapped the boy in.

"Maybe later," Wayne replied.

"Big Bunny," Adam said, reaching back toward his toy, which was still in the van.

"Suppose we leave Big Bunny here?" Wayne asked.

Adam shook his head furiously. "Big Bunny!" he insisted.

"I really don't think it's a good idea to take him," Wayne said, thinking that it would be hard enough to get two kids through security without dragging toys along, too.

Adam began to twist around in the stroller. In less than five seconds he managed to get out of the straps and stood up in the seat. "Big Bunny!"

Wayne sighed. "If I let you take Big Bunny, will you promise to stay in your stroller?"

Adam nodded and slid back down in the seat. A moment later Big Bunny was in his lap and his father was pushing them toward the front entrance of the main building.

Entering the building itself was no problem. It wasn't uncommon for Sterling employees to come in on weekends and catch up on paperwork. As Wayne and Nick pushed the stroller down the empty corridors past labs filled with the most up-to-date electronic technology, Nick couldn't help but feel a wave of excitement. In the stroller, Adam was holding up Big Bunny so he could see everything, too.

"Uh, you know, Nick," Wayne said quietly as they walked, "we'll have to be a little, er, discreet about this."

"Huh?" Nick didn't follow, but before he could ask his father what he meant, a security guard in a gray uniform turned the corner and came toward them.

"Uh-oh," Adam mumbled.

But the security guard smiled when he saw Wayne. "Hey, Mr. Szalinski."

"Hi, Smitty," Wayne replied. Nick thought his father seemed a little nervous.

"Bringing the family around for a little show-and-tell?" Smitty asked.

"Uh, yeah," Wayne replied.

"You're not going to be doing any work today, are you?"

"Oh, no," Wayne said. "I might just tidy up a few things, but that's all."

Nick noticed that the security guard's demeanor changed slightly. The smile on his face seemed a little more forced now. Adam noticed something, too, because he held his nose and pointed at the guard, giving him the "you stink" message. Nick kicked the stroller to get him to stop.

"Well, see you later," Wayne said. He started to push the stroller a little faster than he had before. As they passed the security guard, Nick thought he noticed a look of suspicion on Smitty's face.

A few seconds later Wayne and his sons entered the main lab. As Wayne flicked on the lights and started up the computer banks, Nick looked around in awe. "Wow, this is some lab!"

Wayne smiled. "A lot better than what I used to have in that old attic, huh?"

"Oh, yeah." Nick nodded enthusiastically.

Wayne grinned. "Glad I woke you up early?"

"No," Nick said. "But now that you did, I don't mind as much."

Adam apparently agreed. Wayne had parked him in front of an electronic console covered with bright flashing lights, and the little boy clapped with delight as he watched them blink on and off.

"Okay," Wayne said, rubbing his hands together. "Time to get to work."

"I thought you said you were just going to tidy up a bit," Nick said.

"I am, in my own way." Wayne pointed at a computer terminal. "Think you can handle that?"

"Sure." Nick sat down and cracked his knuckles.

"Good," Wayne said. "Now call up a command directory labeled Primary Laser Drive and tell me what it says under Intensity."

Nick followed the order and typed quickly. A moment later Access Denied flashed onto the computer screen in large yellow type.

"Access denied, Dad."

"Darn." Wayne drummed his fingers against a magnetic recorder. "I'll have to find a way to manually cut down the intensity of the lasers."

Nick watched his father gaze around the room, looking for something he could use to lower the laser intensity. There was an empty soda bottle lying on a table nearby. Nick picked it up.

"Hey, Dad, what about this?" he asked, holding the bottle up and looking through it as if it were a telescope. "Maybe it could diffuse the laser."

"Excellent idea!" Wayne quickly took the bottle and smashed it on the floor, startling Nick and Adam.

"Uh-oh," Adam said warily.

"This is okay, Adam," Wayne said as he kneeled amid the shards of broken glass and picked up the thick round piece that had formed the bottle's bottom. "This could be the only time you'll ever see me approve of breaking something."

Wayne went over to the machine and forced the bottle's bottom into a slot labeled Filter Pack.

"Time to set the final target," Wayne said, thinking out loud.

"But what?" Nick asked.

Wayne looked up and realized there was nothing on the target pedestal to test. Once again he started to look around.

"What are you looking for, Dad?" Nick asked.

"That!" Wayne pointed at Big Bunny. As if sensing what his father wanted to do, Adam tightened his grip on the bunny and shook his head furiously.

"I just want to borrow it for a moment," Wayne said, kneeling in front of the stroller.

"No!" Adam clung tightly to his toy.

"Wouldn't you like to see Big Bunny grow into a much bigger bunny?"

Adam steadfastly shook his head.

Suddenly Wayne got an idea and pulled a pair of dark glasses out of his pocket. "Hey, want to trade for a little while?"

Adam took one look at the glasses and nodded eagerly. Wayne put the glasses on the boy's head and placed Big Bunny on the target pedestal. Then he rushed back to the computer bays behind the machine, hoping to complete the operation before Adam got tired of the glasses and asked for Big Bunny back.

On a private tennis court not far away, Charles Hendrickson stood at the service line and bounced a ball with intense concentration. His opponent was Gil Lemie, a well-known Las Vegas dermatologist and one of the toughest tennis players in the state of Nevada. Hendrickson had never beaten him, but right now the score in games was 5–4, in his favor. One more point and Hendrickson would accomplish a goal he'd been after for years.

He bounced the ball again and then started to toss it in the air for his service.

Tweet, tweet! The cellular phone on the table beside the court rang. Hendrickson stopped his service motion. The ball he'd tossed in the air bounced off his head.

Why now? Hendrickson thought angrily. *Why now!*

"Sorry, Gil. I better get that," he said, walking off the court and picking up the phone. "Hendrickson here."

"Uh, Mr. Hendrickson, it's Smitty down at the lab. Sorry to bother you, but something's going on here I think you should know about."

"And what would that be?" Hendrickson asked.

"Szalinski came in here a little while ago. He was acting nervous, and I thought it was kind of unusual, him being here on a Saturday."

"I see." What the devil could Szalinski be up to?

"I hope I didn't interrupt anything important," Smitty said.

"No, no," Hendrickson replied. "You did the proper thing. Thank you, Smitty."

Hendrickson pressed the disconnect button on the phone and turned to his opponent. "Sorry, Gil. Maybe we can finish up later." Then he turned and walked quickly toward his car. He was on the verge of becoming the head of Sterling Laboratories, and he didn't need that idiot Szalinski messing things up for him now.

Wayne gave a series of urgent commands to Nick, who keyed them into the computer as fast as he could. Around the room images of Big Bunny from various angles appeared on computer screens. The digital clock flashed 00:30.0 and counted down as the Szalinski II began to warm up, whirring and humming. Nick and Wayne slipped on dark glasses. They were so involved in the experiment that they didn't notice that Adam had squirmed out of the stroller again.

"Big Bunny go bye-bye," Adam said.

Wayne's eyes were riveted to the long columns of data scrolling up on the computer screens. Nick's attention was on his computer. Neither noticed that Adam had toddled across the platform and was climbing up the steps toward Big Bunny.

Zzzttt . . . Zzzppp! Suddenly there was a tremendous flash!

"Dad!" Nick cried.

Wayne leapt away from the computer bay just in time to avoid the huge glowing arcs of electricity that quickly encircled it.

"Power surge!" Wayne shouted. "Hit the abort switches!"

Nick's eyes raced over the computer terminal. "Where are they?" he shouted back.

The digital clock was still counting down. 00:05 . . . 00:04 . . . 00:03 . . .

"There are four of them," Wayne cried. "Under the red covers!"

Nick quickly pulled up the covers and flicked the switches. Meanwhile, Adam had arrived at the target pedestal and was reaching up to take back Big Bunny.

Wayne stared at the computer screen. "Come on, already!" he cried. "Abort!"

00:02 . . . 00:01 . . .

It was too late. It wasn't going to abort. . . . The machine crackled. Near the target pedestal, Adam felt the pinpoint of red light strike the back of his head. He turned around and stared down the barrel of the Szalinski II.

"Uh-oh!"

The huge burst of a blue electromagnetic wave hit Adam right between the eyes, knocking him backward and to the floor. Next it hit Big Bunny. Frightened, Adam quickly crawled back down the steps and scampered back to the safety of his stroller.

Wayne looked up at the pedestal and saw the last of the blue light encircle Big Bunny and then abruptly disappear. The computer screens went blank, the instrument panels shut down, and the lights stopped blinking. Wayne and Nick glanced at each other and then raced toward the target pedestal. Wayne picked up Big Bunny and quickly looked it over.

"Anything?" Nick asked hopefully.

Wayne shook his head. "Nothing. No change whatsoever."

Nick was disappointed. "Well, you gave it your best shot, Dad."

"Looks like my best shot wasn't good enough," Wayne said with a sad nod. "At least for today."

The door across the room opened and Smitty stepped in. "Excuse me, Mr. Szalinski."

Wayne and Nick looked up.

"Are you aware that your security clearance denies you access to the equipment without Dr. Hendrickson's permission?" the security guard asked.

"Yes." Wayne glanced at Nick and then tucked Big Bunny under his arm. "We were just leaving."

"Well, you know, Mr. Szalinski . . .," Smitty started saying, almost apologetically. But then he thought better of it as Nick passed, pushing Adam in the stroller.

"Yes, Smitty?" Wayne asked.

"Oh, uh, nothing," Smitty said, looking at Adam. "I was just going to say that this kid of yours is sure starting to get big."

Wayne smiled to acknowledge the compliment, but he had other things on his mind. "See you on Monday, Smitty. Come on, Nick, let's get going."

They put Adam back into the car seat and started home. The sun was higher now, and the van traveled faster. Wayne and Nick gazed out at the desert, lost in their own thoughts while in the back, Adam played with Big Bunny.

"Big . . . big . . . big," the little boy chanted gleefully.

"It should have worked," Wayne said to himself as he tapped his fingers against the steering wheel.

74

Nick turned and studied his father for a moment. "Dad?"

"Yeah?"

"How come you have to ask somebody's permission to work on your own invention?"

Wayne felt a twinge and squinted ahead through the glare on the long narrow strip of road. It was a tough question, even a painful one. "Well . . . your dad's now a member of a team, Nick. I'm getting to work with some very talented people."

"But it's your invention," Nick said. "They didn't have the idea. You did."

Wayne pressed his lips together. In a way, he was proud of his son for not accepting that phony excuse. He just wished that, in this one instance, Nick had.

Nick waited for his father to answer. When he didn't, Nick turned and stared at the broad expanse of sagebrush, fencing, and electrical lines. In the back, Adam kept playing with Big Bunny.

"Adam big . . .," the boy said with glee.

.

Wayne pulled the van into the driveway. Without a word, Nick got out and trudged up the front walk and into the house. Wayne watched him with a feeling of dismay. Something was definitely bothering his son.

Wayne got out and went around to the side of the van to get Adam. His younger son was still in his car seat, playing happily with Big Bunny.

"I think Daddy needs to spend some quality time with Nick," Wayne told him as he reached into the van and undid the restraining straps of the car seat. "So this afternoon we'll get you a baby-sitter."

Usually Wayne slipped his hands between Adam and the car seat and lifted the child out, but this time when he tried to slide his hands in there was no room.

Wayne frowned. It truly was amazing how quickly these kids grew. They'd only purchased the car seat a few months ago and Adam had aleady outgrown it. Wayne tried several more times to get a grip on his son. Finally, he gave a good pull.

Adam didn't budge. Wayne felt a sharp pain in his lower back and quickly let go. Ow! That hurt! Wayne stared at his son and tried to make a joke of it. "You've put some weight on, my boy!"

Adam smiled back. "Adam big."

"Yup, and getting bigger every minute," Wayne said. The problem of getting Adam out of the van still remained. If Wayne couldn't get him out of the car seat, perhaps the best approach was to try and get the car seat out of the van. Wayne reached in and released the seat belt that held the car seat in place. Then he carefully and slowly slid the car seat toward the door.

A few seconds later he staggered backward under the weight of Adam in the car seat. Again Wayne's back was in agony, and as soon as he put the seat down he quickly straightened up, pressing his hands into the small of his back.

"I don't understand it, Adam," he groaned. "You sure didn't feel this heavy this morning."

Still sitting in the car seat and clinging to Big Bunny, Adam looked up at his father with his big innocent eyes. Wayne sat down opposite him and placed his feet against the sides of the car seat. Then, taking his son's hands in his, he pushed and pulled at the same time.

Pop! Adam sprung out of the car seat like a cork and tumbled over his father, who fell backward. Wayne quickly got to his feet.

"You okay, little guy?" he asked.

Adam smiled and nodded. "Adam big," he said, picking up Big Bunny. "Big Bunny big."

"I'll say." Wayne smiled back and led the boy through the front door and into the kitchen. "Now, here's what I'm going to do, sport. First I'm going to call the baby-sitter, and then I'm going to fix you an early lunch." Wayne felt a twinge in his back. "Maybe a light lunch, something lo-cal. And then a little later the baby-sitter will come and Nick and Daddy will go out for some quality time, okay?"

Adam wasn't sure he understood all of it, but he nodded anyway. Wayne put him in his high chair.

"Nack! Nack!" Adam pointed at the snack packs of cheese curls and potato chips Diane kept on top of the refrigerator.

"No way, José." Wayne shook his head. "You need something wholesome to eat." But before he fed his son, he started to go through the dozens of pink, yellow, and blue paper slips that were stuck to the refrigerator door, looking for one with that new baby-sitter's name on it.

"Ah, here it is." Wayne pulled a yellow note off the door and dialed the number written on it. He listened to the phone ring.

A few moments later a man answered. "Hello?"

"Uh, hi, I'm calling about baby-sitting," Wayne said.

"Hold on," replied the man.

Still holding the phone to his ear, Wayne opened

the freezer and started hunting for something to feed Adam. He heard footsteps growing louder as someone ran to pick up the phone at the other end.

"Hello?" a breathless young voice said.

"Hi, is this, uh..." Wayne looked at the paper again. "Mandy?"

"Yeah, who's this?" the girl asked.

"Wayne Szalinski. My wife got your name for baby-sitting."

"Oh yeah?" Mandy asked. "Who's your wife?"

"Uh, Diane Szalinski," Wayne said. "She's a real estate agent. I think she knows your mother."

"Could be," Mandy said. "So you need a baby-sitter?"

"Yes, at three-thirty this afternoon," Wayne said. "Are you available?"

Wayne heard a loud crack over the phone as Mandy popped her bubble gum. "Three-thirty? Sounds okay, Mr. Schlitzminski."

"It's Szalinski," Wayne said. "The address is seventy-seven Del Mar Drive."

"Yeah, got it," Mandy said.

"All right, I'll see you then." Wayne was about to hang up.

"Uh, wait a minute," Mandy said.

"Yes?"

"I charge two-fifty an hour, okay?" Mandy said. "That's the basic rate, and it doesn't include stuff like cleaning up or changing diapers. If you want me to do that, the price goes up."

79

"There might be a little of that," Wayne allowed. "But I'm willing to pay."

On the other end of the line, Mandy smiled. "Way cool. I'll be there."

Wayne hung up and turned back to the freezer. Inside were a variety of frozen meals for children. He pulled out the first one he saw.

From his high chair, Adam nodded eagerly as his father popped the frozen dinner into the microwave and set the timer and power level.

"Now, listen," Wayne said. "You sit there and stay out of trouble, okay? Daddy will be back in a second."

Adam nodded obediently, but as soon as his father left the kitchen, he slipped out of the high chair and waddled over to the microwave oven, fascinated by the quickly changing numbers displayed by the LED timer.

"See, Big Bunny?" Adam said, holding up Big Bunny to the clock display. Suddenly a sizzling blue electric haze flowed out of the microwave and enveloped Adam. It felt like someone was tickling him all over, and Adam giggled. The haze surrounded Big Bunny, too.

"Fun." Adam grinned.

Upstairs, Nick sat on his bed, feeling totally bummed. He'd blown the last weekend of vacation. The whole summer seemed like a big waste. He'd set two goals for himself this summer: A) to make new friends; and B) to meet Mandy Park . . . and he hadn't come close to either. It was at times like this that he wished he was still living in that old run-down house back in California. At least then he could fool around with his next-door neighbor Ron Thompson.

Nick let out a deep breath and picked up his guitar. Maybe he could write a song. Something like "My Dumb Bummed Summer." Then he could become a famous rock star, and Mandy Park would fall madly in love with him, and they'd ride together to all his gigs in his tour bus. Nick smirked. It was a great fantasy, but first he'd have to learn to play.

He picked up the guitar, then remembered three strings were still broken thanks to Adam. Nick found a new package of strings in his desk and started to restring the guitar.

There was a knock on the door. Nick looked up. "Yeah?"

"It's your dad."

Nick sighed. "Come in."

The door opened and Wayne let himself in. "How's the guitar coming?"

"Okay. When Adam hasn't broken half the strings."

"He doesn't mean anything by it," Wayne said. "It's just the way two year olds play."

"Maybe there's a house in the neighborhood that needs demolishing," Nick sulked.

Wayne could see his son was in desperate need of cheering up. He slapped his hands together enthusiastically. "How about we go to a movie?"

Nick looked up. "With Adam?"

"No, I've got a baby-sitter," Wayne said. "It'll just be the two of us."

Nick had to admit he was tempted. Even though it meant going in the solar-powered van and being seen in public with his dad, it was still better than hanging around the house all day with nothing to do.

"There's a picture at the Desert Six I'd like to see," he said.

"Great," said Wayne. "Let's go. It'll get our minds off of everything. Know what time it plays?"

"I'll have to check," Nick said, starting to feel a little better. "The number's on the refrigerator."

"Why don't you come down to the kitchen and call from there while I feed Adam," Wayne said.

"Okay." Nick got up and followed his father downstairs.

"And maybe we can have dinner afterward," Wayne said. "I know this great little vegetarian place."

"How about pizza?" Nick asked.

"Uh, if that's what you want," Wayne said, feeling rather magnanimous, "pizza it will be."

As they crossed the living room, Quark raced toward them, nearly knocking Wayne off his feet. The dog sped into the living room and hid under the couch.

"What's gotten into him?" Wayne asked.

"He looks really scared," Nick said, bending down and looking at the trembling dog. "I haven't seen him look like this since that time we all got into alien costumes for Halloween."

"You think something in the kitchen scared him?" Wayne asked.

"Yeah." Nick smiled. "Adam probably."

"You'd think by now Quark would have gotten used to him." Wayne frowned and stepped toward the kitchen. Nick followed. The next thing they heard was a *bing!* Then everything was quiet.

"Sounded like the microwave shut off," Wayne said.

They got as far as the kitchen doorway.

"Omigod!" Nick gasped when he saw what was inside. "I mean, triple omigod! And ten I-don't-believe-its!"

Wayne just stood there, speechless.

Nick looked at his father. "Dad, how . . . ?"

"This morning in the lab," Wayne said in a trembling voice. "Were you watching Adam?"

"He was off to the side," Nick said.

"Think," Wayne said urgently. "At the moment of discharge. Where was he?"

"I was so busy trying to find the abort switch," Nick said. "I mean, I really thought he was off to the side."

Wayne shook his head. "Somehow, I don't think so."

In the kitchen Adam turned away from the microwave and saw his father and brother. A truly big smile came across his face. "Adam big," he said, holding up Big Bunny. "Big Bunny big."

83

Wayne looked at his son in wonder. "He must be six and a half feet tall."

"Uh, don't worry, Adam," Nick said nervously. "Dad's gonna make everything all right."

Adam smiled again.

"Somehow, he doesn't look the least bit worried," Wayne said.

Adam took a step toward them. Wayne and Nick took a step back. Adam took another step, then stopped at the doorway between the kitchen and living room. He practically filled the entire door frame.

"You know what I said about Adam being six and a half feet tall?" Wayne asked as he and Nick backed into the living room.

"Yeah?" said Nick.

"Make that seven feet," Wayne said.

Adam stopped in the living room and jumped up and down, laughing. Several times he just barely missed hitting his head against the ceiling, and various pieces of furniture and children's toys bounced from the floor each time he landed.

"Fun, fun!" Adam laughed as the wooden floor shook and creaked.

"He seems to be enjoying his new perspective on things," Wayne said.

Adam started to pick up one of the heavy overstuffed chairs.

"Put it down, Adam," Wayne said gently but forcefully. "I said, put it down."

Adam slowly put the chair down.

"I don't think they're going to let him into day care, Dad," Nick said.

"We've got to get him back to the lab and analyze the data," Wayne said. "It's the only way we'll be able to figure out how to reverse the process."

He started forward as if he was going to lead Adam out of the living room.

"Uh, one thing, Dad," Nick said, reaching for his father's arm.

"What's that?" Wayne asked.

"You think the guard might get a little suspicious when we walk in with a seven-foot baby?"

Wayne stopped. "Good point."

Like any problem, there were many ways to approach it, but Wayne decided the best thing to do in Adam's case was to disguise it. Leaving Nick with Adam, Wayne quickly drove into town and dashed into Hal's Big and Tall Men's Shop.

Inside, the store was filled with racks of jackets and suits and shelves of sweaters and shirts. A very average-sized salesman in a blue pinstriped suit approached Wayne.

"May I help you, sir?" the salesman asked.

"Uh, yes, I'm looking for some clothes," Wayne said.

"For yourself?" The salesman scowled.

"Uh, no. For a friend of mine."

"Perhaps you'd like to bring him in so we can take some measurements," the salesman said.

"I can't," Wayne said. "I mean, he can't . . . come

85

in, that is. He's very busy—so busy he doesn't have time to shop, so he asked me to shop for him."

"Can you tell me what his size is?" the salesman asked.

"Well, he's big," Wayne said. "I mean, he's tall."

"About how tall?" the salesman asked.

"About seven feet," Wayne said.

"I see," said the salesman a bit dubiously. "And how would you describe his build? Rather long and narrow, I would suspect."

"Well, that's what makes him so unusual, actually," Wayne said. "He's seven feet tall, but he's also very solid. In fact, people often say he's built just like a roly-poly little boy."

The salesman raised an eyebrow. "A rather large roly-poly boy, would you say?"

"Yes," said Wayne.

The salesman selected several sports jackets, but to Wayne they all looked too small.

"Haven't you got anything larger?" he asked once the salesman had shown him everything on the extra-extra-large rack. The salesman thought for a moment.

"Sir, I have one larger jacket, but frankly I think your friend wouldn't want to be caught dead in it," the salesman said.

"Better show me," Wayne said.

"As you wish, sir." The salesman went into a back room and returned with a loud garish-looking brown-and-beige checked sports jacket.

"What's wrong with it?" Wayne asked. It looked perfectly fine to him.

A few minutes later Wayne parked the van in the driveway and ran into the house with a shopping bag.

"Nick?" he shouted anxiously.

"In here, Dad," Nick called from the kitchen.

Wayne dashed into the kitchen and found Nick sitting on Adam's lap, reading him a story while Adam munched on a box of pretzels.

"How's it going?" Wayne asked.

"He likes having me sit in his lap," Nick answered dolefully.

Wayne reached into the shopping bag and pulled out the jacket. "Look, Adam, grown-up clothes, just like Daddy's."

Adam smiled and his eyes twinkled. He stood up and instantly dumped Nick on the floor.

"How would you like to dress just like Daddy?" Wayne asked.

"Adam like," the child said.

"God, Dad, if we put Adam on World Championship Wrestling we'd be millionaires," Nick said as he got up off the floor. He imitated the announcer's nasal voice. "And in this corner, from Las Vegas, Nevada, weighing four hundred and twenty-five pounds, it's Adam ('the Super Baby') Szalinski!"

Wayne was not amused. "Help me get this jacket on him."

* * *

A little while later the solar-powered van again pulled into the parking lot at Sterling Labs. Adam had insisted on sitting in the front passenger seat, and there wasn't much Wayne or Nick could say about it. As they led him toward the entrance of the building, Wayne took a pith helmet out of the shopping bag and placed it on Adam's head. The helmet had mosquito netting that obscured Adam's face.

"You really think this is gonna fool anyone?" Nick asked nervously.

"Just act naturally," Wayne said quietly.

"Yeah, right," Nick whispered. "I'm supposed to act naturally walking with a seven-foot two year old wearing a pith helmet."

Through a small window in the closed door, Wayne saw that the lights had been turned down low. With Nick and Adam behind him, he quietly opened the door, stepped in, and froze. . . .

There, just visible in the middle of the dimly lit room, was Dr. Hendrickson and two lab technicians. Wayne quickly backed out, pushing Nick and Adam out with him, and shut the door.

"What's wrong, Dad?" Nick asked.

"Uh, nothing," Wayne said. "Just stay right here. I'll be back." He took a step, then stopped. "And make sure Adam keeps his face away from the window."

Once again, Wayne stepped into the lab. This time Hendrickson heard him and looked up. "Szalinski!"

"Oh, uh, hi." Wayne pretended he hadn't noticed

Hendrickson before. "I just stopped by to check on some computations in the database."

"Well, you're out of luck, Szalinski," Hendrickson said angrily. "The database has been erased."

The news stunned Wayne. It couldn't be true. The implications were terrible. "Erased?" he stammered. "Are you sure?"

"Yes, I'm sure!" Hendrickson bellowed. "All thirty-eight gigabytes, gone!"

Wayne started toward the computer terminals, then glanced back and noticed that Adam's face was squarely framed by the window. He instantly backed up, trying to block Hendrickson's view of the window. "But that can't be!"

"Yes it can, Szalinski," Hendrickson replied coldly. "Especially if the main controller was trying to compensate laser intensity."

"Uh, compensate what?" Wayne asked innocently, although he already knew the answer.

"For this!" Hendrickson held up the round bottom of the broken soda bottle. "Which you jammed into the filter pack, you idiot, causing a power surge through the entire main-drive system!"

Wayne took a step closer and gulped. The whole thing was his fault, and both he and Hendrickson knew it. He noticed that Hendrickson was staring past him. Wayne looked back. Adam was in the window again! Wayne stepped in front of the window.

"Who's that?" Hendrickson asked.

"Uh, who?" Wayne asked innocently.

"The guy in the hat," Hendrickson said.

"My . . . my Uncle Yanosh," Wayne said.

Adam chose that moment to try to open the door. He managed to open it a few inches, and only Nick pulling from behind and Wayne pushing back against the door with all his might prevented the boy from getting in. Through a crack in the doorway, Adam started babbling baby talk.

"What language is he speaking?" Hendrickson asked.

"Oh, uh, Serbian probably," Wayne said as he strained against the door, trying not to show it. "He's visiting from Yugoslavia."

"I didn't realize Yugoslavs had such large heads," Hendrickson said.

"Well, he's an unusual person," Wayne ad-libbed. "He has an enlarged, er, brainpan. Highly developed. A real genius. IQ tested at two hundred and twenty-five."

"Bah-foom," Adam said.

"Did he say 'bah-foom'?" Hendrickson asked.

"Oh, probably," Wayne said. "It means 'pleased to meet you' in Serbian."

"Oh." Hendrickson waved back at Adam. "And bah-foom to you, too."

They finally managed to shut the door. Wayne knew he'd better change the subject fast. "How long before the system is restored from the backups?"

"It's of no concern to you, Szalinski." Hendrickson glared at him. "As of this moment you're off the project."

Wayne was stunned. "You don't have the authority to make that decision."

"Maybe I don't," Hendrickson said with a shrug. "If you want you can call Clifford Sterling personally and plead your case . . ." Then he held up the piece of broken glass again. "But after this morning's little escapade and the time and money it's going to cost Sterling Labs, I don't think the old man will have a great deal of sympathy. And I'm sure the board of directors won't." Hendrickson paused. "I think it's best if you leave voluntarily and spare yourself the embarrassment of having to be escorted out by security."

Wayne nodded and turned away, defeated.

As Wayne drove his sons home, he wondered how long it would take the lab to restore the lost database. Knowing Hendrickson, he would probably order the lab technicians to start immediately. It was even conceivable they'd be able to re-create the events leading right up to the point that morning when the system had crashed. And depending on how curious Hendrickson was, he might order the technicians to replicate the video images showing exactly what the Szalinski II had last enlarged.

"Adam big, big," Adam said from the back of the van. "Big Bunny big, big."

Nick looked back at him. "Yeah, we know, Adam. Right now you're probably the biggest two year old since the dinosaurs." Then Nick turned to his father. "How come you didn't tell them, Dad?"

"What?" Wayne asked, snapping back from his thoughts. "Tell them about Adam?"

"Sure," said Nick. "At least then they'd know *you* were able to make the Szalinski II work when nobody else could."

Wayne shook his head slowly. "Remember when we made you and Amy promise never, ever to tell anyone that you were accidentally shrunk and lost in the backyard for two days?"

"Yeah?" Nick nodded.

"Don't you know why we insisted on that?"

"Sure," Nick said. "You didn't want everyone doing stories on us and invading our privacy and asking us to go on TV, where we would have gotten rich and famous."

"That's what we told you at the time," Wayne said. "But there was a much more important reason. We were terrified that if the scientists of this world heard what had happened to you, they would have made you specimens."

"Like, put us in jars of formaldehyde?" Nick cringed.

"Not literally," Wayne said as they pulled back into Vista Del Mar. "But undoubtedly you would have undergone hundreds of tests and been the subject of endless observation. Your chances of ever living a normal life again would have been practically nil."

"Well, then what are we going to do about Adam?" Nick asked as they pulled into the driveway.

"I don't know." Wayne put the van in park and looked with determination at their house. "All I know is we have to figure out some way to fix this before your mother gets home."

No sooner were the words out of his mouth than the front door swung open and Diane came out.

"Hi, guys," she waved. "I'm home."

Frozen in terror, Wayne and Nick stared through the windshield at her. They watched as she reached back into the house and pulled out the recently enlarged Big Bunny.

"Do you have any idea where this came from?" she asked.

The next thing Nick knew, his father threw the van into reverse. The van screeched out of the driveway and into the street. Then Wayne jammed it into drive and peeled out, fishtailing down Del Mar Drive and out of sight.

They were on the road again. Wayne was staring bug-eyed out the windshield, his hands gripping the steering wheel so tight his knuckles were white.

"Dad?" Nick was gnawing on the skin next to his thumb.

"What?" Wayne was finding it difficult to breathe.

"Mama. Mama." Adam had turned around in the backseat of the van and was waving good-bye.

"What should we do, Dad?" Nick asked.

"I don't know," Wayne said. "Come up with suggestions."

Nick thought about it. "Well, we could drive to Mexico and hide out. Then we could come back when Adam's bigger."

Wayne glanced at him in horror. "Bigger?"

"I meant, older," Nick said. "Maybe Mom wouldn't notice then."

Wayne shook his head.

"You've got a better idea?" Nick asked.

"Yes." Wayne took his foot off the accelerator. "Honesty. It's still the best policy. I'll just go back and . . . "

"And what, Dad?"

Wayne swallowed hard. "Explain."

Nick had serious doubts, but if that was what his father wanted to do, he figured he should try to be supportive. "Sure. I mean, when you think about it, it's not the first time something like this has happened."

"It isn't?" Wayne asked.

"Well, to our family," Nick added.

"Right," his father said. "So that's what I'll do. I'll just tell the truth, plain and simple."

"And then beg for mercy?" Nick asked.

Wayne nodded. "Exactly."

Five minutes later Wayne steered the van back into the driveway and got out, leaving Nick inside to keep Adam under control while he tried to explain the situation to Diane. Big Bunny rested on the front walk beside her.

"What was *that* all about?" she asked as Wayne walked up the path toward her.

"Huh?" Wayne replied innocently. "Oh, uh, a little

95

problem I've been having with the van lately. I keep going for park and hitting reverse instead."

Diane frowned. Wayne decided it was time to change the subject.

"So, uh, I see you came back early," he said.

"I took a cab from the airport," his wife said. Wayne noticed that she was trying to see inside the van. Only the sun's glare off the windshield stopped her. Wayne tried to divert her attention by taking her arm and turning her toward the house.

"You mean Amy was right?" he asked. "She really didn't need you there?"

"Actually, I felt rather silly," Diane said. She turned and squinted back at the van. "Wait, Wayne. Who's that tall man in the loud sports coat?"

Wayne turned her more forcibly and walked her into the house. "Well, honey, I've been meaning to talk to you about that. You'll get a big laugh out of it."

They stopped in the foyer. Before Wayne started his explanation, he peeked back out at the van, which had begun rocking back and forth as if a struggle were occurring inside. He could just make out the muffled sounds of Adam saying, "Mama! Go see Mama!" and Nick shouting, "No!"

"What is it, hon?" Diane asked with a hint of concern in her voice.

Wayne bit his lip and began. "Well, you know how, sometimes, the things I invent don't always work the way they're supposed to?"

The sound of the van's shock absorbers bouncing and squeaking distracted him. Glancing out of the foyer again he saw that the van was rocking even more wildly than before. Suddenly Diane put her arms around him and hugged him.

"Sweetheart," she said affectionately, "whatever it is, you can tell me. I mean, how bad could it be?"

"Well . . ." Wayne smiled nervously.

Diane kissed him. "After all, it's not like you did something to the kids again."

Wayne felt something catch in his throat. He coughed. Diane thought of something and frowned. "Sweetheart, where are the kids, anyway?"

"Uh . . ." Wayne glanced back at the van. The sounds of grunts and groans and things banging around was louder now. Suddenly Diane heard it.

"What's going on in the van?" she asked.

"The van?" Wayne gasped.

"Yes. And who was that person I saw before?"

"Person?"

Diane turned to her husband. "Why do you keep repeating everything I say?"

"Why? Uh . . . uh . . ." Wayne kept opening his mouth, but no intelligible words would come out.

"Would you please explain this to me?" Diane demanded as she realized something was wrong.

"Explain?"

Exasperated, Diane reached down and picked up Big Bunny. "You could start by telling me where this giant bunny came from."

"Bu-bu-bunny?"

"Wayne!" Diane shouted.

Wayne couldn't stand it any longer. He fell to his knees, begging for mercy. "All right!" he cried. "I confess! I did it!"

"Did what?" Diane gasped.

Before Wayne could explain it, he heard the van's door slide open and the sound of running feet. The next thing he knew, he saw the shadow of a seven-foot-tall figure reach the doorway, its face obscured by the top of the door frame.

"What's that?" Diane gasped, backing away fearfully.

A second later, Adam ducked down and stepped into the foyer. When he saw his mother, a really big smile appeared on his face.

"Mama!" he said.

Diane looked at Wayne with wide, horrified eyes. "Tell me this is some kind of joke," she pleaded. "Please tell me."

But Wayne could only shake his head. "It's no joke. Honey, I blew up the kid."

Diane turned back and stared at her child. No! It couldn't be! Then everything went black.

Wayne just managed to catch his wife before she hit the floor.

"Uh-oh," Adam said as Nick limped up the front walk, disheveled after his struggle with Adam. He peeked into the foyer, but not far enough to see his mother.

"Dad?" he asked nervously.

"Yeah," Wayne said as he kneeled beside his wife and propped her head up.

"How'd Mom take it?"

Wayne looked down at Diane and sighed. "Oh, about as usual."

With Nick's help, Wayne carried Diane to the couch and propped her head up on some pillows.

"Think she'll be okay?" Nick asked, worried.

"In a little while," Wayne said, opening the collar of her blouse.

"She looks awfully pale, Dad."

"So did you when you first saw him," Wayne replied. "By the way, where is he?"

"I don't know," Nick said, looking around.

"Well, you'd better find him," Wayne said.

Nick took a couple of steps, then stopped and smiled. "Know what, Dad?"

"What?" Wayne asked as he fanned his unconscious wife's face with a magazine.

"There's one good thing about Adam being the size he is," Nick said.

"There is?"

"Yeah, he's going to be real easy to find."

Wayne sighed. "Just go."

Loud crunching noises led Nick to the kitchen, where he found Adam ingesting massive handfuls of potato chips and cheese curls from the bags on top of the refrigerator.

"I guess Mom's not gonna be able to keep the snacks on top of the fridge anymore, huh?" Nick said.

"Hungry," Adam said as he finished off the last bag of chips.

Wayne rushed in and grabbed a dish towel. "Mom would be upset if she knew he was eating that junk," he said as he held the towel under the faucet. "It'll ruin his appetite."

"So?" Nick asked as his father squeezed the excess water out of the towel and headed back to the living room.

"Tell him to stop," Wayne said as he patted his wife's forehead with the damp dish towel.

"Are you serious?" Nick called after him. "He nearly killed me in the van because I told him he couldn't go out."

"Look, Nick," Wayne said sternly. "You're his big brother."

Nick looked up at Adam and back at Wayne. "Not anymore."

Wayne realized Nick was right. He heard Adam leave the kitchen and cross behind him. "Where's he going now?"

"East," Nick replied, following his big little brother.

Wayne turned back to his wife, whose eyelids had begun to flutter. Her lips began to move.

"I'll kill Wayne," she muttered deliriously.

"No, no," Wayne whispered gently as he smoothed a few damp strands of hair off her forehead. "You don't want to kill Wayne."

Boom! Boom! Boom! The windows began to shake and pictures on the walls began to sway. Great, Wayne thought in a panic, what a perfect time for an earthquake! He quickly looked out the window. Two women jogged by on the street, and a man walked past with his dog.

They certainly don't look like there's an earthquake in progress, Wayne thought. So what was making those booming sounds? The answer came in a flash.

"Nick?" Wayne called into the dining room. "What's he doing?"

"Jumping on his toys," Nick shouted back.

"Well, make him stop," Wayne said.

In the dining room, Nick watched Adam crush a train set with one blow. Make him stop, he thought in disbelief. Hey, why didn't I think of that? As Adam raised his foot again, this time to smash a large plastic fire engine, Nick cleared his throat and spoke.

"All right, Adam," he said, trying to sound like a gym teacher, "this is your last warning. Stop jumping on your toys."

Adam looked at Nick and then put his foot on the

floor. Nick couldn't believe it. The kid had actually listened? Then Adam smiled mischievously. Instead of smashing the fire engine with one foot, Adam jumped on it with both feet!

Kaboom! Nick was pelted by pieces of the fire truck and little plastic firemen.

"All right, Adam," he said with a sigh. "I'll give you one more warning. . . . "

As Adam kept right on crushing toy after toy, the loud booming noises coming from the house began to attract the attention of the people passing outside. The man walking the dog stopped, as did Patty and Janet, who had stopped on their way back from the party supply store.

"What's going on in there?" Patty asked.

"I don't know," Janet replied. "But he's some kind of inventor, and if he's experimenting with bombs, it could affect real estate values around here."

The man with the dog nodded. "If he's experimenting with a big enough bomb, there won't *be* any real estate values around here."

Janet and Patty exchanged a concerned look.

"Maybe we better go," Patty said.

"No, let's wait," Janet said.

"But we don't have time," Patty said. "We've got to get ready for the party."

"Just for a moment," Janet pointed out.

In the Szalinski living room, Wayne was still trying to revive his wife. He'd given up on the damp dishcloth and was now trying to wake her with smelling salts, which he waved under her nose. Suddenly Diane flinched, opened her eyes, and looked up at her husband.

"AAAAAHHHH!" she screamed.

"Honey, please," Wayne tried to calm her. But the next thing he knew, she grabbed him by the collar, flipped him over on the couch, and pinned him on his back. She crouched above him, her eyes glistening with fury.

"Honey," Wayne said softly. "It isn't as bad as it seems."

"It almost couldn't be, could it!" Diane screamed at him.

At that moment Nick entered the living room and saw his mother straddling his father on the couch. They sure picked strange times to get romantic.

"Excuse me, guys," Nick said.

His parents turned and stared at him.

"Well, I finally got Adam into his room," Nick told them.

"Did you tell him he has to stay in there?" Wayne asked.

Nick nodded.

"Did you close the door?" Diane asked.

"Locked it." Nick smiled proudly.

Suddenly, from above, they heard a crash of splintering wood and then footsteps on the stairs. A moment later Adam toddled into the living room carrying his door under his arm.

"I think Adam just opened his door," Wayne sighed.

Outside the house, a small crowd of neighbors had gathered on the street, attracted by the sounds of the ruckus within.

"We really should go," Patty said.

"Not yet," replied Janet.

"I'm sure it's nothing," Patty insisted. "There's no reason to get distracted by a little thing like some noise."

"Little things have a way of becoming very big things, Patty," Janet replied.

Little did she know. . . .

Inside the house the Szalinskis were playing tug of war with the door to Adam's room.

"Give Mommy and Daddy the door, Adam," Wayne said as he and his wife pulled on one end.

"Fun, fun," replied Adam as he pulled on the other end.

"You have to be more firm with him," Diane told her husband. Then she turned to Adam. "It's not supposed to be fun! This is a door, not a toy! Now let go, Adam!"

Adam could tell his mother meant business. He let go of the door, and his parents promptly fell backward. As they scrambled to their feet, they watched in horror as Adam stumbled backward and sat down hard in one of the dining room chairs. *Crunch!* The chair collapsed beneath him.

"Uh-oh. Faw down," Adam said as he got back to his feet and looked down at the splintered chair.

"At this rate he's going to destroy the entire house!" Diane gasped as Adam wandered off toward the pantry. "Oh no! Watch out for the china closet!"

Crash! So much for the china. Diane ran after her son, hoping to stop him before he did any more damage.

"Come with Mommy, Adam," she said, grabbing his large, pudgy hand and pulling him back into the living room.

"Let's play in here," she said in her patient mommy's voice. Then she glanced at Wayne and added, "Daddy will play with you."

"What am I going to play with him?" Wayne asked.

"Play anything!" Diane replied sharply.

Nick came in with one of Adam's record albums. "This'll distract him."

While Nick put the record on the stereo, Diane noticed that Wayne had pulled down all the living room shades.

"I don't want the neighbors looking in," explained Wayne. "God forbid they should realize there's a seven-foot baby in here. The *National Enquirer* will be breaking the door down."

No sooner were the words out of his mouth than the doorbell rang. Diane and Wayne exchanged terrified looks.

"Don't answer it," Diane said.

"I have to." Wayne moved toward the front door. "Whoever it is knows we're home. The van is in the driveway."

He peered out through the peephole.

"Who is it?" Diane whispered behind him.

"The neighbors," Wayne whispered back.

The doorbell chimed again. This time Adam noticed.

"Doorbell! Doorbell!" He started to waddle toward the front door.

"No!" Wayne, Diane, and Nick shouted all at once. Nick rushed back to the stereo and turned the volume up loud. A moment later, "The Hokey Pokey" blasted out of the speakers.

The music diverted Adam's attention from the door. Wayne and Nick quickly pulled the giant baby into their circle and started dancing while Diane went to the front door and opened it slightly. Outside were two women in jogging clothes. Diane had noticed them once or twice around the neighborhood.

"Yes?" Diane smiled pleasantly.

"We heard shouting and a lot of noise and noticed the curtains were drawn," said Patty, who was craning her neck to see inside the house. "We were just wondering if . . . "

"If what?" Keeping the plastic smile on her face, Diane moved slightly to block Patty's view.

"If everything is all right," Patty said.

"Oh yes," Diane said. "Everything's fine. We were just entertaining . . . uh . . . "

While doing "The Hokey Pokey" with Adam, Wayne had kept one ear on the conversation Diane was having at the door. So he knew she needed some help.

"Uncle Yanosh," he said.

Diane flinched, then quickly regained her smile.

"Uh, yes, we were just entertaining Uncle Yanosh."

"From Yugoslavia," Wayne said.

"From Yugoslavia," Diane repeated, amazed at the insanity of what she'd just said.

Patty and Janet were both doing their best to look around her and into the living room. Inside, the dancers had reached the part of the song that instructed them to put their whole body in the circle. That was Adam's favorite part. He leapt into the center of the circle with a massive thud that shook the floor and made the light fixtures rattle. A framed family portrait fell from the wall with a crash. At the front door, Janet and Patty gaped at each other.

"Those Yugoslavians." Diane grinned nervously. "They sure love their Hokey Pokey. Anyway, thanks for your concern. I'd love to stay and chat, but Uncle Yanosh will be insulted if I don't dance with him."

Diane closed the door and pressed her back against it. She slowly counted to three to give those nosy women time to go back down the front walk. Then she stared incredulously at her husband, who was still dancing. "Uncle Yanosh? From Yugoslavia?"

Wayne shrugged sheepishly.

"Are you out of your mind?" Diane screamed.

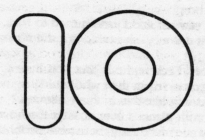

Wayne sat hunched over the dining room table. Before him lay a sea of sheets from a yellow legal pad, covered with complex calculations. He was working feverishly to try to understand what he had done to Adam ... and more important, how he could undo it.

Behind him in the living room, Adam sat in a hastily erected giant-sized version of the Auto-Tend Playpen. Like its smaller cousin in Adam's room, this Super Auto-Tend displayed a number of attention-getting devices for Adam to play with, including mirrors, noisemakers, large swirling disks of color, and clown heads on springs.

The Super Auto-Tend Playpen had several new features, including Nick and Diane Szalinski, who raced around it shaking large rattles made of plastic juice pitchers containing whole walnuts. They wanted to keep Adam entertained and out of trouble.

"Woo, woo! Adam!" Diane danced about in front of her son, who watched indifferently. "That's my big, uh, boy."

Adam yawned and Diane turned to Nick.

"If you ask me," she said, "it's still a playpen to him."

"Maybe," Nick replied. "But you have to admit, there aren't too many guys who could have whipped up something like this in thirty minutes."

They both glanced over at Wayne, who was still hunched over the dining room table, scribbling. Not only was the table covered with yellow sheets, but yellow balls of crumpled paper lay around his feet as well. As they watched, Wayne studied a sheet carefully, then shook his head in disappointment and ripped it in half.

"Darn," Wayne muttered.

"Having a problem?" Diane asked.

"Problem?" Wayne's smile was as phony as the one Diane had given the neighbors. "Oh, no. . . . No problem at all."

"Hey, Adam," Nick was saying, "leave the clock alone."

Diane spun around in time to see Adam reach over the side of the giant playpen toward the large ornately carved antique cuckoo clock that hung on the wall. The clock had been in her family for generations and was known to be extremely valuable. "No, Adam! No!"

"Coo-coo." Adam's fingers strained over the top of the pen toward the clock.

"Don't hurt the cuckoo, Adam!" Diane cried.

Adam's fingers closed around the clock, and he pulled it into the playpen. As Diane watched in horror, her son shook the clock, making the tiny wooden cuckoo pop in and out.

"Cuckoo, cuckoo, cuckoo."

The harder Adam shook, the faster the cuckoo came out through the little door until *sproing!* it popped out and dangled by a slowly uncoiling spring.

"Oh no!" Diane shook her head, heartbroken.

Adam held the broken cuckoo clock close to his eyes and frowned. Deciding that it was no longer fun to play with, he let it drop to the floor with a thud.

Diane picked it up. She had hoped to leave it to her children someday. She turned sadly to Wayne, who was so deeply immersed in his calculations that he hadn't noticed what had happened. Suddenly Diane's anger flared. She knew she shouldn't blame her husband, but darn it, if he'd only been more careful in the lab that morning, Adam would still be a normal-sized two year old.

"Listen." Diane angrily dropped the remains of the clock on the pad in front of him. "When you get a second, you might take a look at *this*."

Wayne focused on the clock and then stared up at his wife with a hurt, mystified look on his face. As Diane sensed his own frustration, she felt her anger melt away. Her inclination to vent her anger by yelling passed into a realization that it was time to talk seriously. Diane glanced back to check on Adam and saw that Nick had gotten his attention and seemed to be promising him something. In the momentary calm, Diane took the opportunity to sit down beside her husband and rub his knotted shoulder muscles.

"Feel better?" she asked soothingly.

Wayne nodded. "A little."

"What about the calculations?"

"Well, I think I've made some progress," he said. "It looks like the answer might be in the atomic, uh . . . Well, some of the numbers indicate . . . "

"Tell me the truth," Diane said. "No more scientific jargon."

Wayne heaved a sigh. "The truth is, without access to the data at the plant, there's not much I can do. I know what's happened, but I don't know why."

Diane let go of his shoulders and gazed down at the floor in despair. Now it was Wayne's turn to touch her gently on the shoulder. "I'm sorry, honey."

Neither of them seemed to notice that for the first time in hours, Adam was sitting quietly in his playpen. When Nick came over to tell his parents how he'd calmed his brother, he found them both staring despondently into midair.

"Hey, Mom, Dad," Nick said, trying to cheer them up. "I found a way to keep Adam quiet. Look."

Diane looked up. Nick was holding a family-sized box of ice-cream pops.

"But it's empty," Diane said, not comprehending.

Two-year-old Adam Szalinski peers out of the special playpen that his father invented.

Wayne Szalinski's version of the family car: a solar-paneled van

Fourteen-year-old Nick Szalinski's summer job is selling refreshments at the Wet 'n Wild Water Park.

Mandy Park—the girl of Nick Szalinski's dreams

Wayne prepares to test his latest invention—a matter-enlarging device—on Adam's Big Bunny.

Wayne and Nick forget to keep an eye on baby Adam, who walks right into the path of the enlarging beam!

Diane suspects trouble when she finds that Big Bunny has quadrupled in size!

Nick stares in disbelief at the outline made by his fourteen-foot-tall baby brother.

It's a long way down from the pocket of 112-foot-tall Adam's jumper.

People run for cover as the gargantuan Adam toddles past them.

Wayne and Diane, along with Wayne's boss, Clifford Sterling, look on nervously as Adam wreaks havoc in Las Vegas.

Adam balances what he thinks is a toy car on a neon sign—but it's a real car, and Nick and Mandy are trapped inside!

A kiss from Mandy makes the whole ordeal worthwhile for Nick.

"Well, that's the point," Nick said.

In the Super Auto-Tend playpen, Adam issued a substantial and very contented burp. Diane looked up and stared at him. His face was smeared with chocolate.

"There were twelve ice-cream pops in there," Diane snapped angrily. "You've ruined his appetite."

Nick was shocked by his mother's angry response. "Not necessarily, Mom," he tried to explain. "At his body weight, he should be able to metabolize . . ." He stopped talking. His mother was giving him a look that could've melted glass. "Maybe I should just shut up about it."

Diane stared at her older son and sighed. She knew Nick was only trying to help. The same was true, of course, of Wayne. But it was becoming painfully obvious that this was a problem none of them could solve alone. They needed help, and there was only one place where they could get that help.

"Okay, boys," she said, standing up. "We're going out."

"What? Where?" Wayne asked.

"I'm taking Adam to the lab, Wayne," Diane said. "Hopefully there are people there who—" She caught herself and stopped, but it was too late. Her husband knew exactly what she was about to say.

"Who know what they're doing?" He finished the sentence for her.

"I didn't mean it that way," Diane said apologetically.

Wayne and Diane stared at each other. They both

knew there weren't too many other ways she could have meant it. Worse yet, it was said in front of Nick. Wayne glanced over at his older son, who averted his eyes. It was pretty obvious that his family's faith in his scientific abilities was nearing an all-time low.

"I'm sorry, Wayne," Diane said in a feeble attempt to salvage the moment. "But all I want right now is to see my baby shrink down to his normal size."

Wayne nodded slowly. Diane turned to Nick. "Come on, help me get Adam out to the van."

As his wife and son started back toward Adam, Wayne, feeling frustrated and bewildered, watched them. It was amazing to him how everything had gotten so out of control. All he'd done was create a machine that should have been a wonderful scientific advancement. Instead it had created nothing but problems for him and his family. It was at moments like this that Wayne wished he could go back to the old dusty attic in that little wooden house in California, back to the days before he'd made the mistake of inventing the world's first shrinking machine.

Wayne blinked. Shrinking machine! Why hadn't he thought of that sooner!?

"Honey!" he cried, jumping up from the table. "Wait!"

Nick and Diane turned and stared at him quizzically.

"I've got an idea!" Wayne said excitedly.

Diane looked sad. "I'm sorry, Wayne. But this just isn't the time—"

"No, no, listen!" Wayne said. "It's my machine!"

"We know it's your machine, Dad," Nick said. "That's not the point."

"Yes it is!" Wayne cried. "I'm talking about my original machine! The Szalinski One. They have it stored in the lab's security warehouse!"

It took a moment, but then Nick's jaw dropped. "You mean, like, use the original machine to shrink Adam back down to his normal size?"

"We know it works," Wayne said to Diane.

"All right!" Nick gave his father a high five.

Wayne turned to Diane. "Listen, honey, you have to give this idea a chance."

Diane had to admit the idea had some potential. "I'm listening."

"It'll have to be a covert operation," Wayne said as he headed toward the door. "Diane, you'll have to come with me. Nick, you stay here with Adam."

"Leave them alone?" Diane suddenly stiffened. "Absolutely not. It's out of the question."

"You have to listen, Diane," Wayne beseeched her. "We can't take Adam to the lab. There's no telling what Hendrickson will do if he gets his hands on the child! Do you want to see your son become a research specimen?"

"You're exaggerating, Wayne," Diane said. "Adam's just a baby. No one's that cold-blooded."

"Better believe it, Mom," Nick warned her. "I saw the guy myself. He's a major bodily orifice."

"But not to a baby." Diane couldn't imagine leaving Adam again. The chances of something going wrong in her absence were too great. They all looked in the child's direction. The excitement of the afternoon had finally gotten to Adam, who yawned and rubbed his eyes.

"Look at him," Wayne said. "It's been a long day, and he's exhausted. He'll probably nap while we're gone."

Adam reacted as if he'd just received an electric shock. His eyes went wide, and he jumped to his feet. "No!" He stamped his feet, and the whole house shook. "No nap! No! No!"

"What did I tell you about the *n* word?" Diane reminded.

"Okay, okay," Wayne whispered. "But you can see how tired he is. It's only a matter of time."

Once again Wayne started explaining why his idea was better than taking Adam to the lab. Adam watched warily as his parents quietly conversed.

Finally Diane had to admit her husband's idea made sense. "Well, it's true. Once you get him to take an N-A-P he usually does stay down for a while."

It took some doing, but they finally got Adam to lie on some blankets they'd spread on the living room floor. Even as he rubbed his eyes and started to suck his thumb, he was still trying to fight the idea of sleep.

"No nap," he whined petulantly as Wayne stood in the doorway and sang "Alouette."

"Now, Adam," Diane said gently. "Behave."

"No!" Adam kicked over a table, and a lamp crashed against the wall.

"Stop it, Adam!" Diane raised her voice and placed her hands on her hips.

Adam saw that his mother meant business. "Saw-wee, Mama," he whimpered.

"Now, be a big boy," Diane said.

Adam yawned and finally lay still. "Adam big, big."

"Yes," Diane nodded. "But even big boys need to rest."

A few minutes later Diane and Wayne tiptoed into the kitchen, where Nick was waiting.

"Did it work?" Nick asked.

"He's out like a light," Wayne whispered as he and Diane headed toward the door.

Diane hesitated. "Do you really think this is a good idea?"

"I'm telling you, it'll be fine," Wayne assured her. "We'll be back in less than an hour."

"Go, Mom," Nick said. "This is the best shot we've got."

Diane paused in the doorway and gazed back into the living room. "I hope you're right, Nick." She turned and left, closing the door quietly behind her.

Nick sat down in the kitchen and started to thumb through a magazine. As long as Adam was asleep, he had nothing to worry about, right? Right. But as Nick tried to read, something nagged at him. Some little voice in his head kept saying that if he were

117

a really good big brother he wouldn't be sitting there reading a magazine, he'd be in the living room, keeping an eye on Adam through this long and difficult vigil.

Nick put down the magazine and quietly tiptoed into the living room. Adam was lying on the floor, his eyes closed, breathing rhythmically. Nick wondered if he needed a blanket. It wasn't cold or anything, but it just seemed strange to see his brother lying there in his clothes. Finally he decided to go down to the linen closet and get a light blanket. He returned and gently spread it over his sleeping brother. But Adam was so large now that Nick couldn't get the blanket over his shoulders and feet at the same time.

For a moment Nick wondered if he should go out to the garage and get the car cover, but then he thought better of it. Instead he took a seat on the couch and watched Adam sleep.

Don't you worry, big guy, he thought. Everything's going to be all right.

Dr. Charles Hendrickson sat at his desk at Sterling Labs and launched another paper airplane at the wastepaper basket in the corner. The floor was covered with dozens of flying paper objects; so far he'd been unable to get any of them to fly straight. As he started to fold another piece of paper, he had to smile to himself. Everything was back on track now. The technicians had spent the day reconstructing the database that was lost when that idiot Szalinski placed the broken piece of glass in the filter pack and caused the power surge. Not that Hendrickson expected to find anything interesting in the reconstructed data, but at least the fact that it had been lost served as the perfect excuse to throw Szalinski off the project, once and for all.

Brinnng! Brinnnnng! His desk phone started to ring, and he answered it. "Hendrickson here. What is it?"

"Uh, sir, it's Moser down at the lab," said the technician on the other end of the line.

"Any developments?" Hendrickson asked.

"Well, sir, we've reconstructed the database right back up to the time of Szalinski's unauthorized use," Moser explained. "And it appears that there was something on the target pedestal."

"So?" Hendrickson asked impatiently. "There've been plenty of things on that pedestal."

"Well, as far as we can tell, and according to the data, there was an actual enlargement."

"Listen, Moser, I'm sure that if you check to see whether it exploded or disintegrated, you'll—"

"Well, we did that, sir. And we haven't been able to find anything to indicate either."

Hendrickson swallowed. "You're telling me that whatever Szalinski did this morning was a success?"

"Well, it sure looks that way," Moser replied.

"Well, my god, man, what was he trying to enlarge?" Hendrickson gasped.

"That's the really strange part, sir," Moser said. "We can't really figure out what the subject was. But whatever it was, it appears to have an unusual number of eyes and appendages. In fact, Drucker here thinks it might even be a new life-form."

Hendrickson couldn't believe what he was hearing. Was it possible that Szalinski had not only managed to get the machine to work but had used it to create some new form of life?

"What does this new kind of life-form look like?" he asked.

"It's pretty hard to describe, sir," Moser said. "I mean, since you're already at the lab we thought it might be best if you came back down and saw it yourself."

"You're darn right I'm coming down there," Hendrickson said. "Don't you move a muscle until I get there."

"We won't, sir," Moser said.

Diane was quiet during the ride to the Sterling Labs security storage area. As Wayne drove, he glanced over at her a few times, wondering what he could say to make her feel better. He couldn't blame her for being upset. After all, what he'd done to Adam could have some very disturbing side effects. For instance, the typical human being matured to a height just about two times his or her height at the age of two. Therefore, if Adam continued to grow at just a normal rate of development, he would probably be more than fourteen feet tall at maturity.

Once again, Wayne glanced over at his wife, who was gazing silently out the passenger window at the desert and the jagged brown mountains behind it. He had a feeling she would not find these thoughts particularly soothing.

In the distance he could see a group of old, large airplane hangars. "That's the place."

Diane turned and looked out the windshield. "We have to look in all those hangars?"

"Just one belongs to Sterling," Wayne said. "The rest are rented by other companies."

As they got closer they saw a hangar clearly marked Sterling Labs. Another sign beneath it said: Warning: Restricted Area. Trespassers Will Be Prosecuted.

Wayne glanced nervously at Diane. He hadn't actually explained to her that he'd been thrown off the project by Hendrickson, but he had a feeling that one of the ramifications was that he would now be considered a trespasser in security areas.

"I think we ought to be sort of stealthy about this," he said.

Diane looked surprised. "Why? You're an employee of Sterling Labs. You have as much right to be here as anyone."

Wayne swallowed. "I, uh, know that. But Sterling stores a lot of other things here besides my machine. And now that they own the license on the Szalinski One, they might not look too kindly on my taking it back."

Diane seemed to buy this explanation, and a moment later Wayne drove around to the back of the hangar area and parked. They got out and started to walk quietly toward the front. Suddenly Wayne heard something.

"Quick," he whispered, grabbing his wife and pulling her down behind some old crates.

A few seconds later a security guard passed, driving a small three-wheeled vehicle. He stopped in front of the Sterling Labs hangar, checked the lock on the door, and then drove on.

"Coast is clear," Wayne whispered, getting up again. They started to inch toward the door.

"Want to know what is the only thing worse than having a seven-foot-tall two year old?" Diane whispered.

"What?"

"Having a seven-foot-tall two year old whose parents are both in jail for trespassing."

Wayne looked back at his wife. He knew she was right, but there was no giving up now.

They tiptoed up to the door, and Wayne quickly entered the security code into the electronic lock. "Okay, honey," Wayne whispered as he pushed the door open. "We'll be out of here in a second. They stored all my stuff in one large crate. It should be easy to spot."

They stepped inside. It took a moment for their eyes to adjust to the dim light.

"Uh, Wayne . . . " Diane found herself staring at a mountain of crates. There were hundreds of them, piled three and four high and running from the front of the hangar clear to the back. Looking up, she saw dozens more in a loft high above.

"Easy to spot?" she said with a groan.

Wayne couldn't believe it. It would take hours—no, *days* to find that crate.

"Maybe they're in alphabetical order or something," he said, grasping at straws.

Diane gave him a very dubious look.

The anger and frustration of the previous few

weeks, and especially the past few days, welled up inside him. Wayne felt his jaw tighten. "Well, it's not my fault. All I wanted to do today was take Nick to the . . . " He remembered something and stopped. The baby-sitter! Oh no!

"What?" Diane asked.

"Oh, uh, nothing." Wayne tried to shrug it off. Diane was already upset enough. He didn't want to tell her that he'd forgotten to cancel the baby-sitter.

Adam slept soundly on the floor of the living room. Nearby, on the couch, Nick had also dozed off, catching up on the sleep his father had interrupted earlier that morning. Even Quark had calmed down enough to take a nap.

Nick was dreaming of the Wet 'n Wild Water Park. Mandy, Barry Lusk, and Robbie Fishman were standing at the base of the Fun Chute. They were waving and shouting at someone.

"Come on!"

"We're rooting for ya, dude!"

In his dream, Nick suddenly realized who they were calling to. . . . It was him! They were waving and shouting at him! In the dream, Nick smiled. All he had to do was go down the chute and he'd join them, be accepted by them, be one of them.

Nick hopped on the chute. The rushing water sent him careening down through curves and around bends. He couldn't see Mandy and the guys, but he could hear their shouts and cheers growing louder and louder.

"All right, dude!"

"Hang in there!"

The smile on Nick's face grew even bigger. In just a couple of seconds he'd splash into the pool. Then they'd all get a couple of sodas from some wimpy concession kid and take off in Barry's jeep.

Nick lay prone in the chute. The flatter you were, the faster the water carried you down. This was it! he thought. This was what he'd waited for all summer! He shot down and splashed into the water, then jumped up to join his friends.

But something was wrong. Mandy and the guys had looks of terror on their faces. They were staring past him and up at the chute. Nick turned around. There was giant Adam, wearing a pair of bathing trunks and shooting down toward them! Mandy and the guys screamed and started to climb out of the pool.

"Come back!" Nick shouted. "It's just my—"

Before he could get the word out, Adam flew out of the chute and hit the pool with an enormous splash.

Nick awoke with a start. For a moment he had no idea where he was. Then it all came back to him. This huge thing lying on the floor was Adam. Nick realized he'd fallen asleep on the couch. Seeing Mandy was just a dream.

Ding dong! The doorbell rang, and Adam started to stir. In a desperate attempt to keep his brother from waking, Nick leaned close and started to sing softly:

I know an old man who had five
    little pigs.
Pigs, pigs high-diddle digs . . .

Ding dong! Darn it! Nick thought. There was no
way he was going to be able to keep Adam asleep
as long as that doorbell was ringing. Nick quickly
tiptoed past his brother.

Ding dong! Ding dong!

"All right, all right," he said.

He reached the door and slowly opened it until
he saw a sliver of long, wavy brown hair and a single
blue eye. Puzzled, he opened the door a little more.

"Mandy?" This had to be a dream. That's it, he
was still sleeping.

"Oh, hi, Rick," Mandy said.

Nick suddenly knew he wasn't dreaming. "It's
Nick. Nick Szalinski."

"Right."

"So what's up?" Nick asked, trying to be cool.

"I'm here to baby-sit," Mandy said.

What! Nick thought. Then he remembered. He
and his father were supposed to go to the movies.
His father had said something about calling a baby-
sitter. But now that Adam was seven feet tall, all bets
were off.

"Gee, I'm sorry, Mandy." He hated saying this.
"But we really don't need a baby-sitter anymore."

Thump! Thump! Thump! Nick heard the unmis-
takable sounds of giant baby steps behind him. He

quickly slammed the door in Mandy's face and looked back into the living room.

"No, Adam!" he hissed. "Go back, go back!"

Ding dong, ding dong, ding dong! Mandy was ringing the doorbell again.

"Doorbell," Adam said.

"Yeah, doorbell," Nick said. "Look, stay right there and I'll take care of it, okay?"

Without waiting for an answer, Nick opened the door and slipped out, quickly pulling it closed behind him. Mandy was standing outside, looking pretty annoyed.

"Very funny, Nick," she said sharply. "Now, can I come in?"

"Uh . . . " Nick didn't know what to say.

"Look." Mandy pointed at her watch. "I'm already charging you."

"But like I said, we changed our minds," Nick tried to explain.

There was a loud *thunk!* against the door behind him. Nick backed against it and grabbed the doorknob tightly.

"What I'm trying to say," Nick continued, "is we just don't need a baby-sitter."

Nick felt the doorknob start to turn. He squeezed it even harder.

"And what I'm trying to say is your father called and I'm here," Mandy said. "Look, I need eight more dollars to see Hammer, and your father promised me three hours at two-fifty an hour plus extra if I'm grossed out. Now, if he isn't a total tightwad and gives me a tip, I'm there."

With his hands behind his back, Nick was struggling against the doorknob with all his might.

"Listen, Mandy," he said. "Take it from me. You don't want to baby-sit. Not this baby."

Mandy put her hands on her hips and snapped her bubble gum angrily. "Like, you really think I can't handle some stupid baby?"

Nick felt the doorknob being yanked out of his hands. The door flew open and there stood Adam. When he saw Mandy he smiled his big smile. "Hi, girlie!"

Nick watched Mandy's eyes widen and then roll up into her head. The next thing he knew, she fainted straight into his arms.

"Uh-oh." Adam backed away from the door.

It wasn't every day that Nick found himself standing in the front doorway with the girl of his dreams in his arms. Under any other circumstances, this would have been a dream come true. But right now he just had to get her out of sight.

It seemed to take forever, but Wayne finally found the crate in the loft high above the floor of the hangar. They'd been away from Nick and Adam much longer than Diane had hoped they'd be, and now that they'd found the machine, she knew it would take even longer to get it down. They tied a rope around the crate and lowered it to the floor. Then Wayne sneaked out of the hangar to get the van and back it in. They loaded the crate into the van and began to unpack the Szalinski I.

"But it's all in parts," Diane cried.

"You drive," Wayne said, staring down at the unassembled machine. "I'll stay in the back and put it together."

Diane ran around to the front of the van and got in. Suddenly she realized something.

"Wayne," she said. "This is a solar van, and we're inside."

"It's okay," Wayne said. "I recharged the batteries

last night. There's a switch marked Batteries. See it?"

Diane looked on the dashboard and located the switch. There were two positions: Low and High.

"Just be careful," Wayne was saying. "Make sure you don't switch it to . . . "

In her haste, Diane flicked the switch before Wayne finished the sentence.

". . . High," he said.

Diane looked down at the switch. She'd flicked it just where she shouldn't have. The van lurched forward so quickly that Wayne was thrown against the back doors. The next thing he knew, there was a loud crash as the van smashed through the hangar doors and shot away under the bright Nevada sun. In the front, Diane grappled with the steering wheel as she fought to avoid crashing.

"Do you have control of the van?" Wayne shouted from the back as the vehicle weaved and swerved away from the hangar.

"Oh, sure," Diane shouted back. "I'm always in control."

Not far away, Charles Hendrickson hurried down the immaculate hallways of Sterling Labs. His mind was filled with grandiose thoughts. Somehow that idiot Szalinski had gotten the machine to work, but given Szalinski's poor reputation and the fact that there were no witnesses to the event, Hendrickson was certain it wouldn't be too difficult for him to take the credit. And, according to Terence Wheeler, that would result in his being named head of Sterling Labs. However, if the technicians were correct and Szalinski had somehow also managed to create a new life-form, well . . . *that* was something really worth taking the credit for.

Hendrickson pulled open the door to the lab and rushed toward the two lab technicians, who were still squinting at the computer monitor, trying to decipher the events of that morning. When they saw him coming, the technician sitting at the computer quickly stood up and gave the seat to him.

"All right," Hendrickson said as he sat down. "Now, what's this about a new life-form?"

"Well, I think we were mistaken about that," one of the technicians admitted.

"Yeah," said the other. "After we scanned it more closely, we came up with this."

He quickly keyed in several commands, and the computer monitor responded with a bright new outlined image. Hendrickson squinted. "What is it?"

"We're pretty sure it's a big stuffed bunny, sir," the technician said.

Hendrickson glared at him. "Are you telling me that you mistook a big stuffed bunny for a new life-form?"

"This is just the beginning, sir," said the other technician. "If you watch the screen, you'll see that about two point three seconds before discharge, something pretty startling occurred. That's right about here."

The technician pointed, and Hendrickson stared

at the screen. It appeared as if the outline of a little boy stepped in front of the bunny and looked squarely into the video monitor. Then *bzzzzt!* the screen went to snow.

"That was the power surge?" Hendrickson asked.

"We're pretty sure, sir," the technicians replied.

Hendrickson felt beads of sweat on his forehead. "How old would you say that boy was?"

"Well, I have a two year old at home," one of the technicians said. "And he's built an awful lot like that."

"Doesn't Szalinski have a child that age?" Hendrickson asked.

The technician nodded. "Come to think of it, I think his kid and my kid are at the same day-care center."

"But there's no indication that the boy's size changed." Suddenly Hendrickson remembered something positively startling. "My god!"

The technicians exchanged concerned glances. "What is it, sir?"

"Uncle Yanosh!" Hendrickson gasped.

"Uncle who?"

"Quick," Hendrickson gasped. "Where does Szalinski live?"

"I think he's got a place over in that new community, Vista Del Mar, sir," one of the technicians said. "You need directions?"

But Hendrickson was already racing out of the lab. He had to pay Szalinski a visit immediately.

Nick turned on the television for Adam. The big child sat on an ottoman in the middle of the living room with Big Bunny, his eyes glued to the set.

"Now, promise me you won't go anywhere," Nick said.

Adam nodded and stared at the screen. Nick felt it would be all right to leave him like that for a few minutes while he tried to deal with Mandy. He went back into the dining room, where he'd left Mandy roped to a chair with a dish towel tied around her mouth. As he entered the room, Mandy stared at him, her eyes wide with fear. Nick wished she wouldn't look at him like that, but under the circumstances, he really couldn't blame her.

"Now, Mandy," he said, "you have to believe me. Everything is under control. I'll take the gag out of your mouth only if you promise me you won't scream."

Mandy just stared back at him. With her mouth gagged he couldn't quite read her expression.

"So, will you promise?" he asked.

Mandy nodded. Nick reached behind her and undid the dish towel.

"AAAAAAHHHHHHHHHHH!" Mandy let out a blood-curdling scream. Before Nick could get the gag back on her, she tipped the chair forward and tried to get away with the chair still tied to her back.

"Mandy! Stop!" Nick shouted as he chased her around the dining room table.

"Help! Giant baby!" Mandy kept screaming. "Giant baby!"

"Please stop it," Nick gasped. "Do you want the neighbors to hear?"

"Yes!" Mandy nodded excitedly. "Help! Giant baby!"

Nick must have chased her for another five minutes before she finally ran out of breath and slumped into the chair she'd been carrying around on her back.

"Man!" she groaned and shook her head in disgust as she gasped for breath. "I've been screaming for five minutes! You can kiss off neighborhood watch around here."

Nick sat down across from her and caught his breath. "Try and understand, Mandy."

"Understand what?" she gasped. "That you've got a giant baby in there? Oh, that's really easy. Sure."

"It doesn't matter what he looks like or what his size is," Nick tried to explain. "He's still a little kid."

"Oh, yeah?" Mandy replied. "Well, you're right about one thing, Rick."

"It's Nick," Nick said. "Really, it isn't that hard to remember."

"Okay, Nick," Mandy said. "Like I was saying. You're right about one thing. There's no way I'm baby-sitting for him."

"Fine," Nick said. "You don't have to. But before I let you go, you gotta try and understand why you can't tell anyone about this."

"Not tell anyone that I just saw a seven-foot-tall baby?" Mandy shook her head. "You're not serious."

"I am, Mandy," Nick said. "Look, you know what he's doing right now? He's sitting in the living room watching TV like any other little kid would. He's not hurting anyone."

"If that's your argument for why I shouldn't tell anyone," Mandy said, "I suggest you come up with something better."

"Okay," Nick said. "I'm gonna tell you a story about something that happened to me and my sister two years ago. Now all I'm asking you to do is listen, okay?"

Mandy struggled against the ropes that bound her to the chair. "Like I have a choice?"

"Well, not really," Nick admitted. "But if you listen, maybe you'll understand."

As Nick started to tell her the story of how he and Amy, and Ron and Russ Thompson were shrunk and lost in his backyard in California, the kid's movie Adam was watching ended. After a couple of commercials, Richard Simmons came on and started jumping around. Adam grinned. He liked watching him and moved closer to the screen to get a better view. Suddenly a blue electrical field burst out of the TV screen, just as it had out of the microwave earlier. As it enveloped him, Adam began to giggle. Once again it felt as if he was being tickled all over.

Back in the kitchen, Mandy could hardly believe her ears.

"You're saying two years ago your father made you and your sister tiny?" she asked.

Nick nodded. "And the guys next door, too."

"And then he made you regular size again," Mandy said. "And now he's made your baby brother big?"

"That's right," Nick said.

"And you don't think that's unusual?" Mandy asked.

Before Nick could reply, loud booming sounds began to come from the living room. They resembled the sounds Adam had made earlier when he'd jumped on his toys, only these noises were much, much louder. The dining room began to shake. Cupboard doors swung open, and pots and pans began to rattle out. Mason jars fell over and crashed to the floor.

"Oh no!" Mandy shouted. "It's an earthquake!"

There was a huge crash in the living room. Nick raced out of the dining room to see what had happened. Adam was gone, and the TV set was lying on its side. A sideways Richard Simmons was imploring the TV audience to get their knees pumping and jog. Nick realized that Adam had taken the request seriously. A trail of broken and overturned furniture led to a gaping hole in the wall nearly fourteen feet high and shaped just like a very large little boy.

Nick swallowed and ran back into the dining room and started to untie Mandy.

"Look," he gasped. "You have to help me. He's getting bigger."

"I'd like to, Rick—" Mandy began to say.

"Nick!"

"Yeah, Nick, like I said. I'd like to, but this really isn't part of my job description."

"My father'll pay you overtime, I promise," Nick begged.

Mandy took a moment to think it over. "Okay, but just one thing."

"What?"

"There is no way I'm changing that kid's diapers."

Sagebrush and cactus raced by as Diane sped back toward Vista Del Mar in the solar-powered van. In the rearview mirror she could see her husband working frantically to piece together the Szalinski I. He was wearing a welding helmet, and every few seconds there was a sharp sizzling sound and a brilliant burst of sparks. Several hours had now passed since they'd originally embarked on this insane mission, and her husband's words kept ringing in her ears. "One hour, tops," he'd said. Oh, Wayne, Diane thought with a heavy heart. I love you, but I wish you wouldn't always make life such a challenge. She looked back at him.

"Wayne?"

"Yeah?"

"How's it coming?"

"I just about have it."

Should she believe him? Did she have any choice? Once again frustration welled up inside her.

"Wayne?"

"Yeah?"

"When this is over, I want you to know, this is it! This is *really* it! No more Mr. Wizard! No more subscriptions to *Popular Science*! I'm not kidding!"

Diane was so busy talking to her husband that she didn't notice the pair of motorcycle cops lurking behind a billboard along the side of the road. As soon as the van shot past, they took off after her. Diane heard their sirens. She looked in the rearview mirror to discover the motorcycles racing up behind, their warning lights flashing.

"Honey?" Wayne said.

"I know, Wayne!" Diane snapped. "I know!"

"I was just going to say that I don't think we can outrun them," Wayne said, as he peered out the back of the van. "Our top speed is seventy-five. I'm sure the police can do better than that."

Diane looked down at the speedometer. They were already going seventy-five miles an hour.

"Wayne?" she said.

"Yes?"

"I think I'm having trouble with this situation."

"I can see that," her husband said.

"How?"

"Any sane person would have pulled over by now," Wayne said.

"If I pull over it will take us forever to get home to Adam," Diane said.

Behind them the wailing of the sirens was growing louder as the cops got closer and waved their arms for her to pull over.

"Any suggestions about what I should do?" Diane asked.

Wayne stared down at the Szalinski I on the floor of the van. It was almost completely reassembled, its barrel aimed out the back. For power, he'd hooked it up to the van's electrical system.

"Keep going," Wayne said. "Maybe it's time to see if this thing works."

He pushed open the back doors of the van. The motorcycle cops were only a hundred feet behind them. Even at that distance Wayne could see them scowl at the sight of the Szalinski I, but before they could take evasive action, Wayne pushed a button.

Zzzzzzzaaaaaaaaapppppp! A wave of blue light burst from the end of the machine, and both cops seemed to disappear.

"Yaaaaahhhhhooooo!" Wayne shouted.

Diane looked in the rearview mirror and saw nothing but empty road.

"I did it!" Wayne shouted. "I did it!"

Diane jammed on the brakes, and the van screeched to a stop. Sometimes she didn't understand Wayne at all. It was one thing to be speeding and try to avoid being caught but quite another to turn motorcycle cops into munchkins.

"Wayne Szalinski!" she shouted angrily. "You unshrink those policemen right now!"

"Do I have to?" Wayne asked.

"Yes!" Diane said. "How do you think their wives and children are going to feel when they find out their husbands and fathers were turned into ants?"

"They might be very happy," Wayne said.

Diane glared at him in the mirror. "That's not funny. Now unshrink them before you get us into real trouble!"

Wayne sighed and aimed the machine at the spot where he'd last seen the two motorcycle cops. Another wave of blue light burst out of the machine and the cops reappeared in their original size.

"Okay, honey!" Wayne shouted. "Let's go!"

The van's tires screeched, and once again they were speeding down the road. Diane kept looking in the rearview mirror for any sign of the policemen.

"Aren't they going to come after us again?" Diane asked.

"I think they've changed their minds," Wayne replied with a smile.

At Janet Beyda's house, several doors away from the Szalinskis', the party for her six-year-old daughter was finally getting under way. Janet had dressed up in a magician's tuxedo with a top hat and stood with her back to the pool, performing tricks for the bored-looking children who sat in a circle before her.

"Now, here's one you've never seen," Janet said, slowly inserting a giant needle through a balloon without making it pop.

"I've got that trick at home," one of the kids shouted.

"Yeah, anyone can do that!" shouted another.

"Boo, boo," the kids protested.

Brats, Janet thought, but she kept a smile on her face. "Okay, kids, maybe you have seen that one, but not this one."

"Oh, sure," one of the kids grumbled.

"Yeah, I bet," said another.

"Just shut up and watch," Janet snapped as she tapped a wand against the rim of the top hat. "All right, boys and girls, watch carefully..."

As Janet started to perform the trick, making a rabbit appear, the children's eyes bulged and their jaws dropped. Finally, she thought, I've got these little suckers.

"Now, who can tell me where the bunny is?" Janet asked.

Not a single child could respond. They all looked completely stunned. Wow, I must be pretty good, Janet thought. Maybe I could do this for a living. Suddenly the kids jumped up and started to run away.

"Hey, wait!" Janet shouted.

Patty was coming out of the house carrying a tray of paper cups filled with fruit punch. The children raced past her, with looks of extreme terror on their faces.

"What's gotten into them?" Janet asked.

As Patty turned toward her, her jaw dropped. And

so did the tray. Janet couldn't understand what was going on.

"All I asked them to do was tell me where the bunny is," Janet tried to explain.

Still unable to talk, Patty lifted a trembling finger and pointed past Janet. Janet turned and looked up at something that resembled a baby boy holding a stuffed rabbit and climbing toward them over a stone wall that separated their yard from the next-door neighbor's. The only thing that seemed slightly out of the ordinary was the fact that the wall was six feet high and the boy appeared to be fourteen feet tall.

"Hi," Adam said with a really big smile. He held up Big Bunny. "Big Bunny," he said.

Janet's eyes went wide and her mouth fell open. She took a terrified step back . . . and fell right into the pool.

As Dr. Charles Hendrickson raced toward the Szalinski home in his car, he shouted loudly into his car phone, "I don't care if Clifford is at the Rand Institute this weekend! I want him notified! And . . . uh . . . I also want the board of directors in on this!"

Without warning, a whole pack of kids came racing into the street. Hendrickson dropped the car phone and jammed on the brakes, skidding to a halt and just narrowly avoiding hitting several of them.

What the devil? he thought, angrily rolling down

his car window and shouting, "What's wrong with you kids!"

No one stopped to answer him. Hendrickson was just about to put the car back into gear when he saw something bobbing behind the house from which the kids had just come. He rubbed his eyes and looked again. No, he thought, it can't be! A second later Adam came around the side of the house.

Hendrickson's trembling hand reached again for his car phone. With shaking fingers he somehow managed to dial Sterling Labs and get one of his technicians.

"Contact the federal marshals!" he gasped. "Get everyone out to Vista Del Mar immediately! I want the neighborhood sealed off! And get some heavy equipment—something large enough to hold . . . to hold something large!"

Hendrickson hung up and got out of the car. He watched in disbelief as the fourteen-foot-tall boy toddled across the front yard, pulling a giant stuffed rabbit along with him. So Uncle Yanosh was still growing! There was no doubt in Hendrickson's mind that this was Szalinski's kid, the one he'd seen earlier in the reconstructed database.

Adam strolled down toward the curb, accidentally uprooting a tree and kicking over a fire hydrant, which sent a huge spout of water high into the air. He bumped into a light pole, bending it over at a precarious angle. A couple of older kids had been playing kickball in the street, and when they saw

Adam they ran. The ball rolled under a car, and Adam flipped the car over to get it. Then he sat down in the middle of the street, playing happily with the ball.

By now almost everyone in the neighborhood was aware of the giant child in their midst. Seeing that he was seated in the middle of the street playing happily, and sensing that he meant no harm, the residents of Vista Del Mar started to gather around him, marveling at this wonderful freak of nature.

But to Nick, Adam was neither a freak of nature nor an object of curiosity. Wanting only to protect his little brother, he and Mandy ran across the street. Suddenly Hendrickson stepped in front of him. "Hold it right there, son."

Nick recognized the man from the lab. "Get lost, dirtbag." He tried to get around him, but Hendrickson grabbed his arm and held tight.

"I'm afraid you're in the hands of the authorities now," Hendrickson said.

Nick looked down at the hand squeezing his arm. "Yeah," he said, "I can see that."

Meanwhile, they heard sirens in the distance. Soon a whole cavalcade of marked and unmarked police and government vehicles started streaming into the community, followed by one large truck. Mandy sized up the situation and took a step away from Nick.

"Where are you going?" Hendrickson asked.

"I'm not with him, okay?" Mandy said.

Hendrickson smiled knowingly. "You are now."

145

* * *

By the time Diane and Wayne reached Vista Del Mar, the street had been cordoned off to traffic. Dozens of official vehicles were parked haphazardly on the curb and on lawns, their emergency lights flashing. Official-looking men and women with plastic identification badges on their lapels were interviewing people, taking measurements and samples of grass and dirt. The one thing obviously missing from the scene was a large young boy named Adam.

The van skidded to a halt. As Diane and Wayne jumped out and ran toward their house, they could see the boy-shaped hole in its side. Wayne was just about to pull open the front door when Charles Hendrickson stepped out.

"Who are you?" Diane asked, winded by the sprint.

"I am Dr. Charles Hendrickson," Hendrickson replied.

"Oh yeah?" Diane caught her breath. "Well . . . WHERE ARE MY BOYS?" she screamed.

"There's no reason to shout," Hendrickson said with a smug look.

A man in a dark suit joined them. He held a squirming Quark in his arms. Behind him were two more men also wearing dark suits.

"Who are you?" Wayne asked. "And what are you doing with my dog?"

"Federal Marshal Preston Brooks, sir," the man said. "I found your dog hiding in a garage down the street."

"Well, let him go," Wayne said.

Brooks glanced quizzically at Hendrickson, who nodded. The marshal let go of Quark.

"What about my children?" Diane demanded.

"They're quite safe, Mrs. Szalinski," Brooks said. "We needed to give the baby some room so he wouldn't hurt himself."

"Of course," Hendrickson added with a malicious smile, "the mutated child will have to undergo immediate testing."

"Why you . . ." Wayne lunged for the scientist's throat. Unfortunately several marshals grabbed him before he could wring Hendrickson's neck.

It was growing dark, and inside the Szalinski house, Wayne looked dismally around the living room. Not only was there a huge hole in the wall, but the entire room, including his Super Auto-Tend Playpen, was a wreck. He wondered why the TV was lying on its side.

Sitting next to him on the couch, Diane glared at U.S. marshal Brooks and Dr. Charles Hendrickson. "I have a right to know where you've taken my children," she said angrily.

"Just relax, ma'am," Brooks replied.

"Relax?" Diane shouted. "I'd like to see how *you'd* relax if a bunch of bureaucratic morons came along and kidnapped your children."

"Now, ma'am," Brooks said patiently, "that kind of language isn't necessary."

"On the contrary, *sir,*" Diane said sharply, "it appears to be the only way I can make myself understood."

"I think what my wife is trying to say is that our son, even if he is quite large, is still our son," Wayne tried to explain. "He's done nothing wrong, and you really have no right to take him away from us."

Diane watched as Brooks glanced questioningly over at Hendrickson. For the first time in hours she felt a little bit encouraged. They seemed to be getting through to him.

"And our older son has done absolutely nothing wrong," Wayne added. "He's just tried his best to protect his younger brother."

Brooks turned to Hendrickson. "I think they've made some good points, Dr. Hendrickson. What do you think?"

Hendrickson gazed at the Szalinskis. "I'm afraid I have to insist that these two be taken into custody."

Wayne and Diane looked at each other in complete shock. Even Brooks looked surprised.

"You can't!" Wayne sputtered. "On what charge?"

"Theft,'" Hendrickson replied. "Also, malicious mischief, child endangerment—"

Before he could continue, he was interrupted by a flash of headlights in the driveway. Through the window, Diane could see the outline of a long black limousine.

"Excuse me," Hendrickson said, getting up. "That's someone I have to talk to."

They watched Hendrickson straighten his tie and stride out through the front door.

"Who's that?" Diane whispered.

"Clifford Sterling, I think," Wayne whispered back.

"Oh, great," Diane said sadly. "Now we'll *never* get Adam back." She bent her head and stared at the floor. Wayne put his arm around her shoulder and tried his best to soothe her.

Through the window, they watched a tall, lean, and impeccably dressed man get out of the back of the limousine. He had silver hair and a commanding presence despite his advanced age, which Diane guessed to be somewhere around seventy-five.

From inside the living room they could hear snatches of the conversation between Hendrickson and Sterling. Sterling was saying something about an experiment getting out of control. He seemed angry.

"Clifford, I hardly know what to say," they heard Hendrickson reply apologetically. "I tried to warn you about Szalinski from the very beginning."

Diane turned and stared at Wayne with wide eyes, incensed. "Are you going to let him say that about you?" she whispered harshly.

"Wait," Wayne whispered back. "Let's hear what Sterling has to say."

"You did warn me, Charles," they heard Sterling reply. "And if it's any consolation to you, the board of directors believes you were right all along."

Wayne jumped up off the couch.

"You can't go out there!" Brooks said, rising from his chair, but Wayne dodged him and raced out to the driveway.

"Wait! Dr. Sterling!" Wayne rushed up, startling the older man. "You have to believe me, sir. I can reverse my son's growth."

"You can?" Sterling's eyebrows went up. He looked doubtful.

"All I ask is for a chance," Wayne begged. "I know I can do it."

But before he could explain how, Brooks came out of the house and grabbed Wayne from behind by the collar. He was just about to drag Wayne back inside when Clifford Sterling raised his hand.

"Wait. He deserves a chance to speak."

"Thank you," Wayne said, shrugging out of the marshal's grip. "Sir, I'm certain I can get him back to normal."

"With what, Szalinski?" Hendrickson asked contemptuously. "Soda bottles? Maybe a little chewing gum and twine?"

"Who do you think you are, talking to him like that?" Diane shouted as she joined them.

Wayne spun around. "Diane! Let me handle this!" Then he quickly turned back to Hendrickson. "Who do you think you are, talking to me like that?"

But Hendrickson ignored him and turned to address Sterling again. "Clifford, the situation demands that I bring in people who have the expertise *and* the credentials—"

"All right!" Wayne cut him short. "So I'm just some guy from California who tinkered with crackpot ideas in the attic. But let me tell you something." Wayne shifted the focus of his words to Clifford

Sterling. "Sir, this country is standing on the shoulders of people who tinkered on crackpot ideas in attics and basements and backyards! Alexander Graham Bell, working in his two-room flat! He was just one of—"

"Young man!" Clifford Sterling cleared his throat angrily. "Don't presume to stand there and lecture me about great minds and great inventors. Whatever I've been over the years, I have never been a fool ... or been involved with anyone who is. And ..." He seemed to be addressing Wayne directly. " ... I refuse to start now."

Sterling paused to catch his breath and then turned to Hendrickson. "Charles ..."

"Yes, Clifford?" Hendrickson replied.

"You're fired," Sterling said.

A stunned silence filled the air. Hendrickson looked shocked. Wayne was certain he hadn't heard Sterling correctly.

"I-I don't understand," Hendrickson stammered.

Sterling nodded gravely. "Yes, that's precisely your problem."

"You can't be serious," Hendrickson said in disbelief.

"Don't tell me what I can or can't be," Sterling replied.

"But what did I do?" Hendrickson asked.

"I suggest you take some time and think about it," Sterling said. "I have a feeling you'll have lots of opportunity to do just that in the near future."

Hendrickson's eyes narrowed and his jaw jutted

out as he clenched his teeth in anger. The look of shock on his face slowly changed into one of hate. He turned and glared one last time at Wayne, as if to say, "I'll get you for this." Then he turned and stormed away.

The Szalinskis and Clifford Sterling watched him stomp down to the curb where his car was parked. He jumped in, slammed the door, and roared off into the dark.

"So much for that." Clifford Sterling removed his jacket and threw it into the back of the limousine. Then he rolled up his sleeves and gave Wayne a determined look. "Now tell me what you have in mind so that we can get that kid of yours back to normal size by bedtime."

Diane and Wayne stared at each other with looks of disbelief that slowly turned into expressions of pure relief.

Had the Szalinskis known what was happening out in the desert a few miles away, they might not have felt so relieved. There, rolling along a dark highway, was a small caravan of sedans followed by a very large yellow truck with a yellow and black Wide Load sign on it.

Nick and Mandy were passengers in the backseat of the sedan directly in front of the truck. In the front seat were two U.S. marshals. Nick was convinced that Mandy must hate him for getting her involved in this mess. Still, he couldn't help glancing quickly across the seat at her in the dim hope that she'd somehow forgive him. For a second their eyes met, and then they both looked away. Nick could only sigh. Once again, if it had been under any other circumstances, he would have been thrilled to be riding in a car with her. But under these circumstances, given the choice, he would have preferred that the whole thing had never happened.

He turned around and stared back into the double headlights of the big truck following them. It pained him to think of Adam inside, being transported like a shipment of fish or something. Jeez, he thought, even cattle trucks had holes in the sides so the cattle could look out and see where they were going. When he just couldn't stand it any longer, he leaned forward.

"Listen, you guys," he said to the two marshals sitting in the front. "You really can't keep my brother in that truck."

"Don't worry," said one of the marshals. "It's all fixed up inside. As far as your brother's concerned, it's one big playpen."

"That's even worse!" Nick tried to explain.

"I'd listen to him if I were you," Mandy chimed in.

"Look, miss," the marshal said, "when I want your opinion, I'll ask for it."

Mandy's eyes narrowed. She and Nick glanced at each other again. Only this time, they didn't look away until Nick noticed that the highway had begun to run parallel to a line of huge steel electrical towers that must have come from Hoover Dam. He'd never seen such massive towers in his life. As the truck behind them began to run alongside the towers, an almost invisible arc of bluish electromagnetic waves seeped out of the high tension lines and encircled the truck.

Inside, Adam had been lulled to sleep by the movement of the truck. But as the electromagnetic waves surrounded and tickled him, he began to giggle and grow again. Soon his feet were pressing against the truck's back doors and his head was butting against the front of the cargo area. The uncomfortable, cramped position caused him to wake up. At once, Adam, who hated feeling restricted or penned in, decided he didn't like where he was. He straightened his legs, driving them right through the back doors.

In the truck's cab, the driver felt the truck shake and thought he heard a smashing sound. A second later the truck began to rock violently from side to side. The driver fought the wheel for control, but it was no use. The truck careened off the road.

The first hint Nick had that something was wrong was when he noticed that the marshal driving the sedan was staring in the rearview mirror for an unusually long time. Nick turned around just in time to see the truck veer off the road. By the time he shouted "Stop!" the marshal had already slammed on the brakes.

As the sedan skidded to a stop, Nick saw the truck tip over on its side and disappear into a cloud of dust behind them.

"You kids stay here!" the marshal shouted as he

and his partner jumped out of the car and ran back toward the truck.

Nick looked at Mandy. "Do they really expect us to do that?"

"If they do," Mandy replied, "they're a lot dumber than I thought they were."

A split second later Nick and Mandy were running back down the highway behind the marshals, toward the overturned truck. As the cloud of dust started to settle, they could see that the truck's tires were still spinning. The driver had pushed open the door and was crawling out of the cab. The only thing Nick could think about was Adam. If he'd been hurt in the crash, Nick swore he'd kill these guys.

Nick and Mandy reached the marshals just as they began to question the driver.

"What happened?" one of the marshals asked.

"I don't know," the driver said. "Everything was going along fine, and then I heard a crash, and the next thing I knew the truck just went out of control."

"Do you think your brother's okay?" Mandy asked Nick.

Before Nick could answer, a loud creaking sound started to come from the truck. As they watched in amazement, the metal roof of the truck began to balloon out, as if something inside was pushing it. Suddenly there was a very loud *rrriiipppp!* and the whole roof of the truck was peeled back like the top of a tin of sardines. A moment later they watched in stunned amazement as Adam crawled out, got to his feet, and stretched.

"Yeah," Nick said. "I think he's okay. Looks like he's grown a little more, too."

"I'd say he's about four times the size he was before," said the marshal standing next to them. "Maybe even bigger."

The marshal cupped his hands. "Okay, kid!" he shouted. "By the authority vested in me by the U.S. government, I order you not to move!"

Adam frowned and stepped toward them. The marshal started to cup his hands around his mouth again.

"Uh, excuse me," Nick said.

The marshal turned to him. "What?"

"You really think he's going to listen to you?" Nick asked.

"I'm a U.S. marshal," the marshal replied.

"Yeah," Nick said, pointing at Adam. "And he's two years old and about five stories high. Think about it."

The marshal thought about it. "Yeah, I see your point."

"I'm his brother," Nick said. "There's a chance he might listen to me. It's not much of a chance, but I think it's the best shot we've got."

The marshal nodded, and Nick and Mandy stepped closer to Adam, craning their necks to look up at him.

"Hey, Adam!" Nick waved, and his brother looked down and smiled. "How about sitting down, okay?"

"Uh, Nick, do you really think that's such a good idea?" Mandy asked nervously.

At first Nick didn't understand. Then he got it. "Oh, don't worry, Adam wouldn't sit on *us*."

"You sure?"

Nick looked up at his huge baby brother. "On second thought, maybe we ought to back up a little," he said.

Nick and Mandy began to back up. Suddenly they saw two huge pudgy hands reaching down toward them.

"What's he doing?" Mandy asked nervously.

"I don't know." Nick gulped. "But I think it's time to run!"

But before they could, Adam scooped them up.

It was Saturday night, and the offices at Sterling Labs were dark and quiet. Even the most dedicated workaholic technicians and scientists had gone home. In the large laboratory where the Szalinski II was kept, Dr. Charles Hendrickson paced the floor, the tapping of his shoes on the slick tiles echoing around the large room. He stopped and gazed up at the Szalinski II, its cold metal shining dully in the dim light. No, it wasn't Szalinski's machine, it was his. And Hendrickson knew if he played his cards right, after tonight the whole laboratory would be his as well.

A door squeaked open behind him, and a second set of shoes tapped on the polished floor. In the dim light Hendrickson made out the figure of Terence Wheeler, his ally on the Sterling board, walking swiftly toward him.

"You've heard the news?" Hendrickson asked.

Wheeler nodded and looked around. "Are you alone?"

"Yes."

"Where's the kid?"

"I sent him to another lab for atomic analysis," Hendrickson said.

"Amazing," Wheeler said, shaking his head. "Szalinski finally got his machine to work, and what does he decide to blow up? His own kid."

"Szalinski's an idiot," Hendrickson said.

"Now, what's this about you having words with Clifford Sterling?" Wheeler asked.

"It's worse than that," Hendrickson said. "I didn't want to tell you over the phone because you never know who might be listening in. But the truth is, the old man thinks he's canned me."

"Are you sure that's what he said?" Wheeler looked shocked.

"Plain as day." Hendrickson nodded. "He said, 'Charles, you're fired.'"

"He had no right," Wheeler said.

"Wait, it gets better," Hendrickson said. "I don't know this for a fact, but I strongly suspect that his objective is to find the kid and return him to normal size."

Wheeler looked appalled. "This is the first time the machine's ever been used successfully, and he wants to undo the results."

"The old man's getting soft," Hendrickson said. "You get to be his age and you start to feel your mortality."

"Maybe I could understand that," Wheeler said. "But we're talking about a discovery that could make this company hundreds of millions of dollars. We have an obligation to the shareholders."

Hendrickson nodded. He happened to know that after Clifford Sterling, Wheeler held the second largest block of company stock. "*You* have an obligation to the shareholders, Terence," Hendrickson corrected him. "I'm no longer with the company."

"The hell you're not," Wheeler sputtered. "As far as I'm concerned, you're not fired! Not by a long shot. This is the opportunity I've been waiting for. Clifford Sterling's gone too far this time!"

Hendrickson smiled slightly but brought his hand to his mouth so that Wheeler wouldn't see it.

"The board is getting together tonight," Wheeler went on. "Until then, I want you on this! Whatever it takes, just get the situation under control."

Hendrickson nodded. This was exactly what he'd hoped Wheeler would say. In anticipation, Hendrickson had already decided on what he needed. "To accomplish our goals, I believe I'll require military cooperation."

"I have friends high up in the Nevada State Militia," Wheeler said. "I'll arrange for clearance."

"I appreciate your support and faith," Hendrickson said. They shook hands, and Terence Wheeler started away, but halfway across the lab he stopped and turned.

"Charles," he said. "Handle this for us and we'll do the right thing by you."

"I know you will," Hendrickson replied, feeling a great deal more confident than he had before.

The solar-powered van raced through the night, following the same roads the convoy carrying Adam had taken earlier. Inside, Diane drove, with Brooks sitting beside her. Quark sat on the floor at the marshal's feet. In the back of the van, Wayne crouched with Clifford Sterling next to the Szalinski I.

As Diane raced to catch up with the truck carrying her son, Brooks pressed a mobile phone to his ear, trying desperately to reach the marshals leading the convoy.

"I think I've made contact!" Brooks yelled.

"What do they say?" Diane asked.

"It's hard to hear," said Brooks. "The connection's not good."

"Stick the phone out the window," Clifford Sterling said in the back. "These blasted mobile phones are terrible inside cars."

Brooks rolled down the window and stuck his head out.

"What?" Diane heard him shout as the wind raced in. "You've got a what?"

Brooks listened for a moment and then pulled his head in. "They've got a problem."

"What kind of problem?" Diane asked apprehensively.

"I couldn't quite get that," Brooks admitted sheepishly.

"Well, my god, man, get your head out that window and find out," Clifford Sterling ordered.

Brooks leaned out the window again. Diane heard some unintelligible yelling, and then the marshal pulled his head in again.

"What is it?" Diane asked.

"I've got bad news, ma'am," Brooks said solemnly. "Your son's escaped."

"Oh, God," Diane moaned.

They rode in silence for a moment. In the back, Wayne and Clifford Sterling shared a meaningful look. Then Wayne turned toward the front of the van. "Look, maybe that's not so bad. At least he's not in the truck anymore."

"Well, that's part of the problem," Brooks admitted. "He escaped because he got bigger."

Diane bit her lip and gave him a worried look. "How much bigger?"

"I didn't ask," Brooks said.

"Can you find out?" Sterling asked.

"I'll try." Brooks stuck his head out the window again. After a few moments he pulled himself back in. He didn't look happy.

"Well?" Wayne asked.

"No one knows exactly how big your son is now," Brooks said.

"Yes, yes?" Clifford Sterling said impatiently. "Come on."

"All they know," the marshal continued, "is that he put your son and the girl in his pocket and left."

163

"He did what!" Diane screamed. The van started to swerve off the road.

"Easy, easy!" Wayne shouted. "Get control of yourself, Diane."

Diane straightened the van out and stared over at Brooks. "Tell me you're not serious."

"Sorry, ma'am, I'm afraid I am."

"He put them in his pocket." Diane shook her head wearily. "He's always doing that. I find the strangest things in his pockets."

"At least *they* know where he is," Wayne said, trying to look at the bright side.

"If being out in the middle of the desert means you know where you are," Diane added glumly.

"I think the first thing we have to do is try to understand what is causing this growth phenomenon," Clifford Sterling said. "Any ideas, Wayne?"

"I don't know." Wayne scratched his head. Then something occurred to him. "Wait a minute. Did they say they were transporting him along Copper Mine Highway?"

"Yes," Brooks said. "It's about three miles ahead of us."

"Aren't there high voltage lines running alongside it?" Wayne asked.

"There were the last time I drove it," Brooks said. "They run straight from Hoover Dam."

"I made his lunch in the microwave today," Wayne said.

"I don't see the connection," Diane said.

"I left him alone in the kitchen," Wayne admitted.

Diane glared at him. "Wayne Szalinski, how many times have I told you never to leave that child alone in the kitchen? You know he gets into everything."

"Wait a minute," Brooks said. "What's leaving the kid alone in the kitchen have to do with his size?"

"I'll explain in a second," Wayne said. "Now remember when we got home? The TV was lying on its side."

"And we know the boy grew between the time you put him in the living room pen and the time he, er, broke out," Clifford Sterling said.

"Then that's it!" Wayne said excitedly.

"I don't get any of this," Diane said.

"Your son's growth is being caused by electromagnetic flux," Clifford Sterling said.

"What?"

"Listen, Diane," Wayne tried to explain. "Around every operating electrical device there's a flux."

"It resembles an electromagnetic force field," Clifford Sterling added.

"And that is what's making him grow," Wayne explained.

"So when he was around the microwave and the TV he got some of this electromagnetic flux and got larger," Diane said.

"Exactly."

"But from what we've heard it sounds like he got much larger when he was close to those high tension lines," Diane said.

"Well, that would be true," Clifford Sterling said. "The stronger the electrical current, the greater the flux, hence the greater the effect it would have on him."

Marshal Brooks had been quiet up until now. But there was something bothering him.

"Uh, excuse me," he said. "But this electromagnetic flux thing. Would it surround neon lights, too?"

"Absolutely," Wayne replied. "Why?"

"Well, because the direction your kid is going in," the marshal said, "is going to take him straight to Las Vegas."

Diane stared, panicked, at her husband. "Wayne, please tell me there's some kind of limit . . . that he can't just keep getting bigger and bigger."

"I wish I could, honey," Wayne replied sadly.

It was pitch-black, and something was going *ka-thump! ka-thump! ka-thump!* very loudly. At the bottom of Adam's giant pocket, Nick couldn't see, but he knew Mandy had to be nearby. Once again Nick realized he was living a weird variation of one of his most cherished dreams—to be alone in the dark with Mandy Park in the middle of the night.

Ka-thump! Ka-thump! Ka-thump! It was Adam's heart.

"Mandy?" Nick said.

"Yeah?"

"You okay?"

"Just great, Nick."

Ka-thump! Ka-thump! Ka-thump!

"Nick?"

"Yeah, Mandy?"

"Don't let anyone tell you your brother doesn't have a big heart."

Nick had to smile, even if she was being sarcastic.

"I kind of feel like we're at a rock concert," he said. "Sitting in the first row, right in front of the drums."

"I wish," said Mandy.

"So what do you want to do?" Nick asked. "I mean, within the context of being in a pocket about four stories off the ground?"

"Well, I think I'd feel a little better if I could at least see you," Mandy said. "It's kind of scary sitting here all alone."

"Uh, okay." Nick started to crawl across the bottom of the pocket toward her. He came across rocks that must have once been grains of sand and big wads of soft fuzzy stuff that could only have been lint, once upon a time. Suddenly his hand touched something sticky.

"Oh, gross!"

"What?" Mandy asked.

"A gummy bear," Nick said. "Only it's the size of my TV."

He managed to squeeze around it. Next he came to something round that felt kind of granular and porous, with a big hole in the middle. Nick started to crawl over it, but one of his legs fell through the hole.

"Oh, man, is this déjà vu or what?" he groaned.

"Why?" said Mandy.

"I just got my leg caught in a piece of round oat cereal."

"Can you get out?" Mandy asked.

"I'm not sure." Nick struggled to pull his leg back out, but there was nothing to hold on to for leverage. "So far, no luck."

"Here, let me help." Mandy crawled toward him. "Where are you?"

"Just crawl along the bottom of the pocket," Nick said. "You can't miss me."

The next thing Nick knew, he felt Mandy touch his arm. He reached out and grabbed her hand.

"Okay, pull!" he said.

Mandy pulled and he pushed. Gradually he began to work his leg out of the cereal. Suddenly it came free, and Nick tumbled forward onto Mandy. For a moment they were tangled in each others arms, fumbling around, trying to get their balance.

"Gee, sorry about that," Nick said when he finally got his bearings.

Mandy didn't answer. She just smoothed out her hair and sat next to him in the dark.

Ka-thump! Ka-thump! Ka-thump! For a few moments they sat in the dark pocket, listening to Adam's heart.

"Nick?" Mandy said.

"Yeah?"

"What did you mean before when you said it was déjà vu?"

"Well, there's a part of the story I didn't tell you,"

Nick said. "I mean, the story about us getting shrunk. See, the way my father found me was that he almost ate me."

"What? How?" Mandy asked.

"I fell into this bowl of cereal he was eating," Nick explained.

"Was there milk?" Mandy asked.

"Yeah, lots of it," Nick said. "At least from my perspective."

"I always heard milk baths were supposed to be good for you," Mandy said. "But was it scary? I mean, thinking you were going to be eaten by your father?"

"Well, yeah," Nick admitted. "I mean, I wasn't really looking forward to his digestive system, you know."

Mandy shook her head. "Did anyone ever tell you you have a strange but funny way of describing things?"

"Uh, no, but I don't mind," Nick said. "I mean, coming from you, that's almost a compliment."

"Why coming from me?" Mandy asked.

Ka-thump! Ka-thump! Ka-thump! Nick wasn't sure whose heart was beating louder, his or Adam's.

"Well, because you hang out with a lot of people," Nick said nervously. "I mean, you must hear some pretty funny stuff."

"From who?" Mandy asked.

"Like Robbie Fishman or Barry Lusk," Nick said.

"Oh." Mandy thought for a moment. "Well, Robbie's funny sometimes. But what makes you think I hang out with them?"

"I see you with them all the time," Nick said nervously. "You're always hanging out, laughing and everything."

"You mean, at the water park?"

"Yeah," Nick said.

"How do you know I'm always with them?" Mandy asked.

"Like I said, I see you. While I sell sodas."

"Oh, right," Mandy said.

Ka-thump! Ka-thump! Ka-thump!

"I mean, what a drag," Nick said. "There I am, working all summer while you and those guys have this blast. To me, this summer was just a big waste."

"You know what's funny?" Mandy asked. "I feel like it was a big waste for me, too."

"You do?" Nick was surprised.

"Yeah. Like I spent the whole summer hanging out and fooling around. I mean, about the only thing I managed to accomplish was a halfway decent tan that'll be gone before Thanksgiving."

"But you had fun," Nick said.

"Fun?" Mandy echoed. "Yeah, I guess so. I mean, we fooled around a lot, but after a while even that starts to get boring."

"Really?" Nick had never imagined her feeling that way.

"Well, look at it this way," Mandy said. "Barry's a nice guy, but all he can talk about is his jeep. And Robbie's funny, but after a while you know he's gonna do the same routine over and over. I mean, it's fun to hang out with them, but to look back on a whole summer and know the only thing you did was hang out . . . it's sort of a waste."

"So what would you have rather done?" Nick asked.

"Well, that's the funny thing," Mandy said. "I really don't know. Maybe I should have had a job like you do. At least I would've made enough so I could go see Hammer without having to take these dumb last minute baby-sitting jobs."

Nick's mouth fell open. "Oh, wow, I forgot! Are we still paying you?"

"Nick," Mandy said, "if you can get me out of this alive, your father doesn't have to pay me a thing."

The van shot down the highway. Inside, Wayne and Clifford Sterling were still making adjustments to the Szalinski I while Diane drove and Brooks monitored information on the cellular phone.

Then Diane noticed something in the distance. "I see a vague glow up ahead."

"That's Vegas," Brooks said. "We should be coming up to the roadblock pretty soon."

Wayne raised his head and looked shocked. "Roadblock?"

"Yeah." Brooks nodded. "Why?"

"I guess I never thought the day would come when the police would have to set up a roadblock for one of my children." Wayne sighed sadly.

A few minutes later they reached the roadblock, which consisted of a spotlight truck with a gasoline generator, two unmarked police cars, and two police cruisers with the lights flashing. Diane stopped the van near a mobile television truck parked behind the other vehicles. In the distance they could just make out the vague shapes of some of Las Vegas's larger buildings.

"If he heads for the lights, he'll have to come this way," Brooks said as Diane turned off the engine.

Diane turned around and looked at her husband, who was still hunched over the shrinking machine.

"Is this going to work, Wayne?" she asked.

"Absolutely," Wayne replied. "By my calculations, all he has to do is hold still for five point two seconds—"

"*What?*" Diane was certain she hadn't heard correctly.

"Five point two seconds," Wayne repeated.

"You're not serious," Diane said.

"Why not?" Clifford Sterling asked.

"Because he's an active two year old," Diane said. "It's insane to think that he'll hold still for five point *anything* seconds."

Wayne shook his head. "She's right. We had a heck of a time getting his portrait done by a professional photographer. Anything that requires him to be still for more than a sixtieth of a second is practically impossible."

Clifford Sterling rubbed his chin pensively. "I know it seems like a long time, but because of the boy's increased mass, it will require a longer period of exposure."

The van was quiet while Sterling and the others thought about it. "Perhaps we can distract him," Sterling said hopefully.

Their conversation was interrupted by booming sounds in the distance. They quickly scrambled out of the van. Nearby, a woman newscaster stood in the bright glow of lighting set up by her television crew.

"This is Constance Winter reporting live from the sight of what will certainly become the most important news story of the decade," she was saying.

Diane and Wayne exchanged worried glances. This was just the kind of publicity they most wanted to avoid!

Meanwhile, the booming sounds grew louder. They all peered out into the dark, but there was nothing to see.

"Footsteps," Sterling said. A few more seconds passed, and a huge shape began to emerge from the dark. Suddenly the gasoline generator roared on and the spotlight flashed upward, causing Adam to stop short and shield his eyes from the sudden glare.

"Oh my!" Clifford Sterling gasped.

Diane noticed that the marshal standing next to her was looking through binoculars. She quickly grabbed them away.

"Hey!" the marshal shouted. "Those are my binoculars."

"Well, that's my son!" Diane snapped back, bringing them to her eyes and focusing.

"He must be fifty, maybe sixty feet tall," Brooks gasped.

"How's he look, honey?" Wayne asked.

"He . . ." Diane squinted and adjusted the focus again. "He looks like he's okay."

"This is the most amazing thing I've ever seen," Clifford Sterling said somberly.

Diane felt a pang of anxiety. Her knees felt weak, so she leaned against her husband. "Is this going to affect him for life? I mean, couldn't something like this ruin a kid?"

"Now, honey." Wayne tried to reassure her. "It'll probably just give him perspective. Help him see the big picture later in life."

"What about the other kids?" Brooks asked.

Diane quickly scanned Adam's overalls and focused on the pocket. She could just make out two faces.

"I think I see them!" she cried. "Yes! There they are!"

"Nick!" Wayne shouted and waved.

The roar of the gasoline generator supplying power to the spotlight was so loud that it drowned out their voices. Nick didn't hear them. Meanwhile, as Adam's eyes gradually adjusted to the bright lights, he began to look around. Spotting an emergency road sign, he bent down and lifted it straight out of the earth without the slightest effort.

"Remarkable," Clifford Sterling said as Adam lifted the sign to his eyes and studied it.

Near him, Marshal Brooks was conferring with several police officials. Now he turned to Wayne and Sterling.

"I can get rope guns," he said. "We'll shoot ropes over him."

"Absolutely not!" Diane's response had all the ferocious protectiveness of a mother bear. "You're not shooting anything at my baby."

"Baby?" Brooks looked at her like she was crazy. "Look at him! You call that a baby?"

"We're his parents," Wayne said, pushing toward the marshal. "We know how to handle him."

"That's right," Diane agreed.

"Okay," Brooks said. "Then you tell me how you intend to stop him from going to Las Vegas."

Wayne looked up at his son and then across at his wife. "Will you excuse us for a second?" He took her by the arm and gently led her away.

When they were out of earshot, he stopped and spoke in a low voice. "What do you think?"

Diane was still looking up at Adam. "I don't know what to think. What do *you* think?"

"I think we better come up with a plan before they do," Wayne said in a low voice.

There was a crash in the dark behind them. Adam had evidently gotten tired of the emergency road sign and had let it fall to the ground. Not far from Diane and Wayne, the TV news reporter was talking to the camera again.

"What we have just witnessed," she said, "was another act of random destruction by this apparently uncontrollable child."

"It's pretty obvious she's never had kids," Diane fumed.

Wayne snapped his fingers. "That's it!" he gasped. "I've got an idea!"

He ran back to Brooks. "Listen, get on your phone and tell your men I need Big Bunny out here."

Brooks got on the phone. "I need something called Big Dummy."

"It's *Bunny*," Wayne corrected him.

"Make that Bunny," Brooks said into the phone. "No, not Big Dummy Bunny. Big Bunny. Yes, probably near the overturned truck. I don't care what it takes, just get it here fast."

Up in Adam's overalls Mandy and Nick held on to the upper edge of the pocket and looked down at the scene below, shading their eyes from the glare of the spotlight.

"See anything?" Mandy asked.

"Not much with that light in my eyes," Nick answered. He sensed that she was watching him, and he looked back at her.

"You know, Nick," Mandy said. "I'm really glad I met you."

"You are?" Nick was amazed.

"Sure," said Mandy. "Who else would have taken me out for a ride in his little brother's pocket?"

Nick felt disappointed. She was just being sarcastic again.

"Listen, Mandy," he said. "I tried to warn you. I said we didn't need a baby-sitter, remember?"

"I thought you were just trying to blow me off," Mandy said.

"Well, I was," Nick admitted. "But it was for your own good."

"I guess you're right," Mandy said with a sigh. "It's just that no one's ever tried to weasel out of a baby-sitting job before because the baby had become a giant."

"Well, there's always a first time," Nick said.

Suddenly they lurched forward as Adam bent down to pick up a boulder that must have seemed like a pebble to him.

"Hang on!" Nick shouted as he and Mandy almost tumbled out of the pocket. A moment later Adam straightened up again.

Mandy was hanging on to the edge of the pocket, gasping for breath. Her complexion looked slightly greenish in the bright light. "I swear, Nick, I'm gonna barf if he does that again."

Nick stared up, but all he could see was the bottom of his younger brother's chin. "HEY, ADAM!" he shouted. "STOP IT!"

"Like, you think he's really listening?" Mandy observed.

"Just hang in there," Nick said. "I'm positive my dad is gonna come up with a plan to get us."

Down on the ground, Wayne did indeed have a plan. In the distance he heard the faint *whompa! whompa! whompa!* of a helicopter. Brooks pointed toward the west.

"I see it!" he yelled.

Wayne and the others squinted into the night and

spotted the helicopter's single headlight growing brighter as it approached. Soon another object in the sky came into view: a huge tan-and-white bunny suspended by cables beneath the helicopter.

"Big Bunny, ahoy!" Wayne said with a nervous grin.

"I don't like this, Wayne," Diane said. "It's dangerous."

"Got a better idea?" Wayne asked.

Diane shook her head.

Sterling came up behind them. "It's here, Wayne."

Wayne nodded. "Be ready to activate the machine the second he's down."

Sterling nodded and went back to the van. Wayne turned once again to his wife.

"Don't worry." He tried to sound brave. "I'll be fine."

A crooked smile appeared on Diane's face. "You always tell me that."

"And I'm always right, right?" Wayne smiled at her.

When Adam heard the approaching helicopter, he spun around. He caught sight of his favorite toy and began to clap and dance.

"Big Bunny! Big Bunny!"

"Here comes lunch," Mandy groaned, hanging on tightly as the pocket bounced up and down.

"Pick a spot on the horizon and stare at it," Nick said.

"What?"

"Just do it." Nick pointed at the distant lights of Las Vegas. "There. Stare at that."

Adam was still bouncing around. Mandy looked ill. "This is like the worst airplane ride ever!"

"You staring at that spot?" Nick asked, having a hard time holding on himself.

"What? Oh yeah." Mandy forced herself to stare at the distant lights. Meanwhile, down below, the helicopter had landed.

"Is it helping?" Nick asked.

"It is actually, a little," Mandy replied. She turned and glanced at Nick. "How'd you know about that?"

"My father taught me," Nick said. "When we lived in California a friend once wanted to take me sailing, and I asked my father what to do if I felt seasick."

"Did it work?"

"There was no wind that day, so I never had a chance to try it," Nick said. "Now, keep looking at those lights."

Mandy stared again into the dark. "Your father's really smart, isn't he?"

"Yeah," Nick said with some pride. "That's how I know he's got some kind of plan to save us."

No sooner were the words out of his mouth than the two of them spotted the helicopter rising toward them, Big Bunny dangling beneath it.

"Tell me I'm not seeing this," Mandy moaned.

Wayne sat on Big Bunny's head. He was wearing a crash helmet and carrying a bullhorn.

"See," Nick said proudly. "I told you my father would have a plan."

Mandy stared at him in disbelief. "You call this a plan?"

"What do you call it?" Nick asked.

"How about suicide?"

"Well, let's see if it works," Nick said with a shrug.

They watched as the helicopter rose over their heads, bringing Wayne and Big Bunny to Adam's eye level. Inside the helicopter, they could see the pilot at the controls. The copilot had his head out the window and was directing the pilot. As the helicopter slowly moved toward Adam, Wayne raised the bullhorn to his lips and sang.

"That's your father's plan?" Mandy asked in disbelief.

"That's the song he always sings to get Adam to take a nap," Nick explained. "Look! It's working!" They both looked up and saw Adam stick his huge thumb into his mouth and rub his eyes with his other hand.

"They're going to try to get him to sleep?" Mandy asked.

"Yeah," Nick said. "I bet they figure once he's sleeping they can get control of him."

Wayne kept singing. Down on the ground, Diane glanced nervously back at Sterling and the Szalinski I.

"Get ready, Doctor," she said, tensing. "He's getting blinky. He always gets blinky right before he goes to sleep."

181

Up in the air, the helicopter pilot slowly maneuvered the bunny closer to the giant child. With one thumb still stuck firmly in his mouth, Adam started to reach forward to take Big Bunny into his arms. Wayne stopped singing and spoke to his son with soothing bedtime words. Nick turned and smiled at Mandy. It looked like his father's plan was going to work!

"That's right, Adam," Wayne said gently through the bullhorn. "Time for a nice long . . ."

On the ground Diane suddenly realized what he was going to say. She instantly cupped her hands around her mouth. "Don't say it, Wayne!"

Too late. Without thinking, Wayne finished the sentence with the word *nap*.

Mandy and Nick heard a loud *pop!* as Adam pulled his thumb out of his mouth.

"No!" Adam shouted, stamping his giant feet. "No nap!" Then he pushed Big Bunny away, causing it to swing back and forth beneath the helicopter like a pendulum under a clock. Above it, the helicopter rocked back and forth precariously in the sky.

"Release the bunny!" the copilot shouted.

"What about the guy on his head?" the pilot yelled back.

"Look, either he goes down alone or we all go down together," the copilot shouted. "Either way, he goes down."

The next thing Wayne knew, he and Big Bunny were plummeting downward. As they fell past

Adam, Wayne leapt toward his son and landed just below his neck.

Below Wayne, Big Bunny hit the ground with a loud *whomp!* Wayne started to slide down the front of Adam's shirt, grabbing wildly at the material, desperately looking for something to hold on to. Finally his hands hit something cold and metallic. One of the buckles to his son's overalls! Wayne grabbed it and stopped sliding. He sighed with relief. For the moment he was safe.

Adam's sudden movement, shoving Big Bunny away, had caught Nick and Mandy by surprise. They'd each lost their grip and had fallen once more to the bottom of Adam's pocket.

"You okay?" Nick asked.

"As well as can be expected," Mandy replied. "So much for your father's plan."

Nick shrugged. "I guess it wasn't nap time after all."

Nick was just about to start climbing back up to the top of the pocket. He looked up and was startled to see his father hanging above him by the brass buckle, his legs kicking wildly in the air as he tried to get a better grip.

"Dad!" Nick shouted.

"Don't worry, Nick," Wayne shouted. "Everything's under control."

"Boy, if this is what he calls under control," Mandy said, "I'd really hate to see what he thinks is out of control."

As if Adam had heard her, he abruptly twisted around and started to move away from the roadblock. The sudden motion caused Wayne to lose his grip and fall inside Adam's jumper.

"Dad!" Nick cried out.

Wayne knew he'd landed between his son's turtleneck and overalls. Once again, he clawed wildly at the material to stop his fall. Finally he felt a loose string and grabbed it, holding on to it the way he would a rope dangling from a cliff.

Nick had lost sight of his father. He was desperately searching for him when Mandy suddenly screamed.

"AHHHH!" She pointed at something jutting out of the fabric behind the pocket.

Nick realized it was his father.

"Dad?" he said. "Is that you?"

"Yes." His father's voice was muffled by the material.

"Are you okay?" Nick asked.

"Yes," Wayne replied, trying to sound confident. "And I want you to know there's absolutely nothing to worry about."

Just then the string snapped, and Wayne disappeared from behind the pocket as he fell downward again.

"Gee, for a second there I felt a whole lot better," Mandy said with a sarcastic sigh.

Wayne was falling, tumbling, flailing downward through his son's clothes. He almost got a grip on the bottom of the turtleneck, but his feet hit the slippery plastic of the diaper and gave out. Once again he started to fall, this time bouncing off the soft baby fat of Adam's leg and getting caught momentarily near the bottom of his son's pants cuff before landing on the roadbed beneath him.

Wayne hit the asphalt and lay momentarily stunned. Then he heard Nick shouting from high above, "Run, Dad! Watch out for his foot!"

Wayne looked up and saw a size 537 high-top sneaker descending toward him. He quickly rolled away, avoiding being squashed by inches, then jumped to his feet and started to run. Behind him Adam accidentally kicked the TV news truck, sending it bouncing into the desert.

At the roadblock, Diane and the others had watched the events unfold with startling swiftness. As her son started toward them, Diane angrily grabbed a bullhorn.

"Adam Szalinski!" she shouted sternly. "You stop this right now!"

But Adam either wasn't listening or didn't hear as he barreled forward, sending another truck crashing into a bridge abutment.

"Adam!" Diane screamed into the bullhorn. "This is Mommy talking! I told you to stop!"

In another few seconds, Adam would be right on top of them. Diane stood her ground, as if refusing to believe that her son would ever run her over. Just as Adam was bearing down on her, Clifford

Sterling grabbed her and pulled her out of the way. A split second later a huge high-top sneaker landed exactly where Diane had been standing.

"I'm afraid that won't do any good, Mrs. Szalinski," Clifford Sterling said gently. "Your son may have become a giant, but he still expects his mommy to be bigger than he is."

Shaking at the thought that her son had almost squashed her like a bug, Diane stared back at the silver-haired man. Could he be right?

Clifford Sterling continued as if he'd just read her mind. "Right now, to him you're nothing more than a little talking doll."

The words took the wind out of her. He was right, of course. Adam had no more reason to listen to her now than he would have listened to a talking ant when he was normal size.

A second later Wayne rejoined the group, and Diane, glad he'd survived the fall, gave him a hug. They all looked up at Adam, who had crossed the roadblock like it was nothing more than a bunch of micromachine toys, and was now headed toward the lights of Las Vegas. Wayne and Diane stared sadly after him, and Clifford Sterling shook his head slowly in the dark night air.

"I hate to say this, folks." He spoke grimly. "But it looks like nothing can stop him now."

Not far from Sterling Labs, the Nevada State Militia maintained a small airstrip. It was a plain, unsophisticated affair, just a few sheet-metal hangars and a small steel hut that served as headquarters. After making several stops at various military installations, Hendrickson arrived at the darkened airport in a jeep. Nearby, a ground crew was in the process of pulling a dark green tarp off a Nevada State Militia helicopter painted in camouflage colors.

Hendrickson parked the jeep near the helicopter and left the radio on. He needed to hear the up-to-the-minute reports on where Adam Szalinski was headed. From across the tarmac, a man wearing a flight suit and carrying a helmet approached him and held out his hand. "Dr. Hendrickson?"

"Yes?" Hendrickson paused to look the man over. He looked like a fellow who knew how to carry out challenging orders. Hendrickson smiled and shook the man's hand.

"I'm Captain Ed Meyerson, Nevada State Militia, sir," the man said.

"I assume you'll be my escort tonight," Hendrickson said.

"That's correct, sir," Captain Meyerson replied. "Can't say I've ever received orders quite like these, though."

"They come from very high up," Hendrickson lied. It was important that Captain Meyerson believe that any hint of insubordination on his part would have the severest consequences.

"Well, yes, sir," Meyerson said. "I imagine they must have. I mean, no offense, sir, but to grant a civilian like yourself absolute authority over my ground crew and the use of this helicopter . . . well, sir, as far as I knew, that was only allowed to happen in cases of national emergency."

"That's very close to what we've got here," Hendrickson said.

"A national emergency, sir?" Meyerson frowned.

Hendrickson thought it best to change the subject. He pointed to a large covered object in the back of his jeep. "I'll need some of your men to unload this device and set it up in the cargo bay of that chopper."

"Right away, sir." Meyerson turned and barked orders at the men who'd just removed the tarp from the helicopter. Several of them pulled a cart over to the jeep and slowly lifted the device out of the vehicle. As they wheeled it toward the helicopter, Hendrickson and Captain Meyerson followed. The men pulled the cover off the object and stopped and stared at it. It looked like a high-tech cross between a standard twenty-millimeter cannon and a ray gun.

"Tell your men to hurry," Hendrickson told Meyerson. "We don't have a lot of time."

Captain Meyerson issued the appropriate orders, and the ground crew quickly started to mount the device in the helicopter.

"Mind if I ask what it is, sir?" Meyerson asked. "Unless it's classified."

Hendrickson smiled. "Not at all, Captain. It's a tranquilizer cannon. Normally used on large animals."

Meyerson looked puzzled. "Well, sir, I know we've got some mighty big jackrabbits out there in the desert, but I didn't realize we needed this kind of artillery to contain them."

"This wasn't designed for a jackrabbit, Captain," Hendrickson replied. "We're talking elephants and various other creatures. It's even been used at sea to do research on whales."

"Bet you have to be a pretty good shot to get one while they're breaching," Meyerson speculated. "Must shoot pretty powerful stuff, too."

Hendrickson nodded, although he hadn't a clue what that stuff was and didn't care either. Still, he enjoyed hearing himself talk. "The cartridges it fires can incapacitate the target in seconds," he said. "It's like a normal injection . . . on a larger scale, of course."

"So just what are we going hunting for tonight, anyway?" Meyerson asked.

Before Hendrickson could answer, the radio in the jeep crackled: "... reports that the child has once more doubled in size have just been confirmed."

"A kid?" Meyerson frowned.

"Rest assured that this is no ordinary child, Captain," Hendrickson said. "What you will see tonight no one has ever seen before. It's the result of a secret science experiment that has gone completely awry."

Meyerson smirked. "Must be another one of those government screwups."

Hendrickson nodded. He watched as Captain Meyerson's men finished mounting the tranquilizer gun and began to load the ammunition. Hendrickson kneeled down, picked up one of the cartridges, and examined it.

"Boy, that's almost the size of a mortar," Captain Meyerson said, a bit nervously. "You said we're looking for some giant kid?"

"That's right, Captain." Hendrickson ran his finger over the cool shiny metal of the shell casing.

"A human kid, only much bigger?" Meyerson asked.

"Bigger and, as a consequence, considerably more dangerous," Hendrickson replied.

"Well, you're not really going to fire that thing at him, are you?" Meyerson asked.

"Let me remind you of your orders, Captain,"

Hendrickson said. "I will need your full assistance."

"Yes, sir, I understand." Meyerson swallowed. "Of course, I can't take off without final clearance."

"That will be coming shortly," Hendrickson said confidently.

Meyerson glanced again at the tranquilizer gun. "I realize it isn't my place to say this, sir, but I have kids myself, and that just doesn't seem like—"

"Perhaps I didn't make myself clear, Captain," Hendrickson interrupted him. "I understand your concern, but the device you see before you is only a . . . last resort."

"Oh." Meyerson gave him an uncertain look. "Well, in that case I guess it's all right."

Hendrickson smiled. "I'm glad you feel that way, Captain."

Ralph and Margaret Mason hadn't been to Las Vegas in seventeen years. But seventeen was their lucky number, and the retired plumber from Indianapolis and his wife had decided to make a junket. Since arriving in Vegas they'd visited all the monstrous new casinos that had been built since their last visit. But what they'd really come to see again was good old Glitter Gulch on Freemont Street, home to a dozen world-famous gambling joints, including the Freemont Casino, the Pioneer Club, and Sassy Sally's, with its huge neon sign of a cowgirl sitting back with her legs crossed, the toe of one cowboy boot pointing up toward the sky.

They had just left Binion's Horseshoe, where

they'd checked to make sure that the famous million dollars in ten thousand dollar bills was still on display, and were strolling toward Union Plaza in the glow of the light bulbs that gave Glitter Gulch its name. All of a sudden Margaret pulled on the sleeve of Ralph's vintage baby blue leisure suit.

"Look at that, Ralph." She pointed a rhinestone-bejeweled finger at a line of four police cars rolling slowly down the center of Freemont Street.

A loud voice burst from the speaker atop the lead police car. "Clear the street! Clear the street at once!"

But seeing no immediate reason to do this, most of the gamblers and tourists, like Ralph and Margaret, either ignored the warning or simply stopped and looked around, puzzled.

"What do you think's happening, sweetie pie?" Ralph asked.

"Don't know, honey bunch."

"I got it!" Ralph had an idea. "Maybe Wayne Newton's in town!"

"They don't do that for Wayne Newton, honey bunch," Margaret said with a shake of her head. "It must be someone bigger."

"Hey, listen, sweetie pie," Ralph said. "Ain't no one bigger than Wayne Newton in *this* town."

Suddenly Ralph felt a huge shadow pass over him. Like everyone else on the sidewalk, his eyes slowly followed the shadow back to its source—a giant the size of a ten-story building, dressed in children's clothes!

"Of course, honey bunch," Ralph swallowed, grabbing his wife's hand, "I could be wrong!"

And with that, screams filled the air as hundreds of tourists fled in every direction.

The van was now part of a small motorcade of vehicles slowly following Adam's path into Las Vegas. There were ambulances, emergency rescue trucks, marshals' sedans, police cars, and the spotlight truck. Wayne and the others gazed out the windows of the van in astonishment.

"Never seen the streets of Vegas look so empty," Brooks muttered.

In the back, Clifford Sterling held a walkie-talkie to his ear, listening to static and emergency bulletins. "They say he's toddling down the center of Freemont Street."

"He's been told a hundred times not to go into the street," Diane fumed.

"It's probably not even a street to him," Clifford Sterling reminded her. "It's more like a brightly lit miniature amusement park."

"If he makes direct contact with one of those lights, there's no telling how huge he'll get," said Wayne.

"You're right," said Sterling. "We've got to get him away from them."

"How?" Diane asked. "With all the lights and activity and things to look at, there's nothing that's going to make him leave."

Wayne bit his lip and looked around. She was

right. It would be impossible to *make* Adam leave. On the other hand ... His eyes focused on an ice-cream truck parked at the curb, obviously just abandoned by its driver. It was exactly like the one Adam had seen just that morning, with a huge chocolate ice-cream bar on its roof.

"Pull over!" Wayne shouted.

"Why?" Brooks asked.

"I think I see something Adam wants more than lights and activity," Wayne said.

The van pulled to the side of the street, and the emergency vehicles behind it followed. Wayne pushed open the door, and he and the others quickly made their way to the truck.

"An ice-cream truck?" Brooks scowled.

But Clifford Sterling understood immediately. "That huge ice-cream bar."

"Right," Wayne said. "All we need is a really big loudspeaker and someone who can drive an ice-cream truck really fast."

"I used to drive trucks in the army," Brooks said. "How fast do you have to go?"

"Say you had a hundred-foot two year old chasing you," Wayne said.

Brooks nodded slowly. "That fast, huh?"

"It's a good idea," Clifford Sterling said. "But we better move fast. If he grows much bigger, I don't think we'll have a chance of controlling him."

"Are you kidding?" Diane said. "We couldn't control him when he came up to my knee."

* * *

Nick and Mandy had climbed to the top of Adam's pocket again and watched as he passed the color-fully lit casinos.

"You've got to admit, this is a pretty interesting perspective," Nick said as they looked down on the hotels and lights and the terrified pedestrians who looked like scurrying ants.

"Maybe," Mandy said sourly. "But I'm just thinking about the trouble I'm going to be in with my parents."

"Why?"

"They said I was never to go to Las Vegas without a chaperon."

Nick looked up at the bottom of his brother's huge chin. "I'd say you're chaperoned."

Mandy sighed. "Look, Nick, I know you're trying to make me feel better and everything, but maybe we should concentrate on getting out of here before your brother sees a car or some other big thing he likes and decides to drop it in his pocket, on us."

Nick searched his mind for an idea. "Hey, I've got it! A really good plan!"

"As good as the 'plan' your father had?" Mandy asked dubiously.

"Better," Nick said.

"Great." Mandy rolled her eyes. "For a second I was worried."

"Here's what we'll do," Nick said, pointing down into the pocket. "We'll pull the thread out of the seam at the bottom of the pocket and use it as a rope to slide down."

"Say what?" Mandy looked at him like he was out of his mind.

"Believe me," Nick promised as he started to climb down inside the pocket. "It'll work."

They got to the bottom of the pocket and started to pull the heavy red thread out of the seam.

"Do you really think this will be strong enough?" Mandy asked, holding a length of it in her hands.

"We'll double it over," Nick said, twisting some of the thread back on itself. "See? Now it's almost the same as mountain-climbing rope."

Just as Mandy reached to feel the thread, Adam suddenly lurched forward as he tripped over an untied shoelace.

"Whoa!" Nick shouted as the pocket suddenly went from vertical to horizontal and then began to tip down, spilling out the cereal and gummy bear that had been inside.

"Hold on!" They both clung to the thread and slid out of the pocket. The next thing Nick knew, they were dangling in the air! Nick quickly looked around and realized that Adam had fallen forward onto his hands and knees in the middle of an intersection.

"Nick, look!" Mandy was pointing down. Half a dozen feet below them in the street was an abandoned yellow convertible.

"Go for it!" Nick let go of the thread and fell into the seat. The car rocked up and down, and he grabbed the windshield for balance. A split second later, Mandy landed next to him. They both slipped down into the seats. Nick was behind the wheel.

"Get going!" Mandy shouted.

Nick stared in a panic at the dashboard. He'd never driven a car in his life or even seen one that looked like this. He quickly started pushing buttons and turning knobs, praying one of them would start the engine. The lights flashed on, the horn blared, the windshield wipers started swiping back and forth.

"Maybe it's this one!" Mandy flicked a button, and the convertible's top started to rise.

The commotion in the car caught Adam's attention. Still on his knees, he reached down and started to push the car back and forth and around in circles. "Zoom! Zoom!"

"What's he doing?" Mandy braced herself against the dashboard as the car was whipped around like a carnival ride.

"Playing cars, I think," Nick shouted. "Better get your seat belt on!"

The van turned the corner and came to a screeching halt. A block away, in the middle of Glitter Gulch, Adam was on his knees, playing with a yellow sports car as if it were a toy. Wayne and the others jumped out of the van.

"Put it down, honey!" Diane shouted. "Put the car down!"

But Adam didn't hear her as he made the convertible go around and around faster and faster.

"It's just a plaything to him," Sterling reminded her.

Now Adam rose to his feet.

"My god!" Sterling gasped.

Diane looked pale and shaken.

"What is it, honey?" Wayne asked.

"You don't realize how big he is until you get this close," Diane said.

"We've got to get these lights off before he touches any!" Sterling shouted.

Wayne grabbed the walkie-talkie and pressed it to his ear. "Brooks!" he said in a rush. "How are we doing with that truck?"

"Almost set!" Brooks's voice crackled back.

"Hurry!"

They watched in awe as Adam pulled a piece of green-and-red hard candy from his pocket, studied it for a moment, and then tossed it away. A second later it crashed through the windshield of an unoccupied car.

"He doesn't even know what he's doing," Diane gasped.

Now Adam looked down and picked up the sports car again, lifting it high into the air.

"ZZZZZOOOOOOOOOOOOOOOOOOOOOM!" he laughed. "Air pane!"

"AAAAAAAHHHHH!" Inside the convertible, Mandy screamed and grabbed for Nick as they suddenly rose a hundred feet off the ground. Nick rolled down the window and shouted as loudly as he could, "It's not an airplane, Adam!"

It was hard to know whether Adam heard him or not, but Nick sensed that the car was being lowered.

"I think he's bringing us in for a landing!" he yelled.

"As long as it's not a crash landing," Mandy groaned with her eyes squeezed shut.

Suddenly they weren't moving anymore. Mandy opened her eyes and looked at Nick, who was staring out the window.

"Did we land?" she asked, hopefully.

"Sort of." Nick was sitting very stiffly and seemed to be having trouble breathing.

"What do you mean, sort of?"

"Look." Nick slowly pointed outside.

Mandy rolled down her window and looked. Her jaw fell open. They'd landed, but not on the ground. Instead, the car was balanced precariously on the upturned toe of the huge neon cowgirl sign outside Sassy Sally's.

Now Mandy was having trouble breathing, too. "H-how far down is it, Nick?"

Nick didn't want to look. "I'd guess fifty feet."

"What happens if the car falls off?" Mandy asked.

"I don't know," Nick replied. "But I have a feeling that even if we had air bags it wouldn't help."

Down the block, Diane saw two heads sticking out of the windows of the car. She grabbed the binoculars and took a closer look. "It's Nick and Mandy! In the car!"

Wayne immediately got on the walkie-talkie again. "Brooks!" he shouted. "You have to wait!"

"What's the problem?" Brooks asked.

"We can't distract Adam now," Wayne said.

In the sports car, Mandy and Nick had become aware that even the slightest move could tip the car in one direction or another.

"Just don't move," Nick said cautiously. "Just wait."

"For what?" Mandy asked. "King Kong to come save us?"

Suddenly a loud blast of ice-cream-truck music blared into the night air. Adam looked away from the car.

"What was that?" Wayne shouted into the walkie-talkie.

"The electricians accidentally crossed the wires," Brooks explained.

"He's going to leave us here, Nick." Mandy started to unfasten her seat belt. "This probably isn't the smartest thing I've ever done...."

"Mandy! No!" Nick shouted. But before he could stop her, Mandy pushed open the car door on her side. Immediately, the car began to tip sideways, and Mandy started to fall out. Nick dove across the seat and grabbed her wrist just before she dropped out of sight.

Nick was stretched across the front seats, both of his hands now wrapped tightly around Mandy's wrist and his foot hooked through the car's steering wheel to keep them both from falling to the street. Mandy dangled in the air beneath him. If he lost his grip on her wrist, she'd fall. And, at any second the car could tip and they'd both go down. It was a long drop to the street below, where a crowd, including Wayne and Diane, had gathered and was looking up at them.

"N-Nick..." Mandy's voice quavered. Her eyes were saucer-sized with terror. "P-please don't l-let go."

"Don't worry." Nick held on to her wrist with all his strength. "My parents are always complaining about how hard it is to find baby-sitters. They'd kill me if I let go."

"Nick!" Mandy gasped. "That's not funny."

"I know. Look, I'm gonna try to pull you up, but you have to help. Okay?"

"Okay."

Nick twisted his head around and looked up at his brother. "Adam!" he shouted, but his brother was still looking around for the source of the ice-cream-truck music.

"Come on, Adam!" Diane shouted from the ground. "Help them! Come on!"

Mandy reached up and grabbed Nick's arm with her other hand and slowly began to pull herself up.

"Good, Mandy," Nick encouraged her. "All right, keep it up."

"I can't believe I'm doing this." Mandy grimaced as she inched up. "I always hated rope climbing in gym."

"This is more like guy climbing," Nick said. Then he twisted around again and shouted, "Adam!!!"

It was useless. Adam wasn't paying any attention. Too much was going on. Nick had an idea. He pushed his foot against the car's horn.

Beeeeeeep!

It worked! Adam actually turned around and looked down at them. "Uh-oh. Faw down."

Mandy had just managed to crawl over Nick and

back into the car, but the shift in weight caused the car to teeter in the opposite direction. Nick heard a scraping sound as it started to slide off the sign.

"Oh no!" Diane covered her eyes as the car began to fall off the sign and hurtle toward the ground.

Nick was experiencing weightlessness for the first time in his life. It would have been interesting if he hadn't been in a car plummeting toward a very hard-looking road surface. Maybe it was the only fitting ending to what had been his first and last date.

Suddenly he stopped falling and felt the car start to rise. Nick stared across at Mandy. Had they crashed and died instantaneously? Were they both on their way to heaven? No, they were in Adam's hand!

"He caught them!" On the ground Wayne and Diane felt a rush of relief and hugged each other. Then Diane pulled away and waved at her younger son. "Okay, Adam. Put them down. Come on . . ."

But instead of putting the car down, Adam was lifting it toward his face.

"No! No!" Wayne and Diane shouted.

The next thing Nick and Mandy knew, they were looking through the windshield into the largest blue eyes they'd ever seen.

"He sees us!" Nick gasped.

"Care-foo, Nick-Nick," Adam said. "Care-foo girlie."

"He's gonna put us down," Nick said hopefully. "I just know it."

Adam started to lower the car, but suddenly Nick and Mandy found themselves turned around and aimed straight down. Adam let go!

"AHHHHH!" they screamed.

A second later they were enveloped in something dark and thrown violently forward as they came to a sharp stop.

On the ground, Wayne's shoulders slumped forward in disappointment. "He put them in his pocket again."

Diane nodded sadly. "He's always been possessive."

It was Sterling who snapped them out of their gloom.

"Come on, folks," he said. "We can't wait any longer. We've got to do something before he grows any larger!"

Wayne picked up the walkie-talkie. "Brooks? Kill the neon and light up the truck. Let her roll!"

A second later, the ice-cream truck, driven by Brooks, pulled out onto Freemont Street with ice-cream-truck music blaring from the speakers. Adam spun around.

Come on, Adam, Wayne prayed, it's your favorite ice cream. As if his prayers were answered, Adam took off after the truck. All along the Las Vegas strip, cooperative casinos shut down their lights so that Adam wouldn't grow any larger as he passed.

"It's working!" they heard Brooks shout over the walkie-talkie.

"Come on!" Sterling ran back to the van. "Let's go!"

Everyone jumped in, and they took off after the ice-cream truck and Adam.

In the front seat of the van, Wayne slapped his hands together. "I knew it would work! He's a sucker for ice cream."

But his joy was short-lived. Once again the walkie-talkie crackled on, only this time Brooks didn't sound so jubilant. "Where are you guys?" he cried. "This kid's gaining on me!"

It was too easy to imagine the ice-cream truck racing along at top speed and Adam racing up behind it. Wayne floored the van, and they shot toward the edge of town. But it wasn't long before they came to the truck parked on the side of the road, with Brooks sitting glumly in the driver's seat.

The van pulled up next to him, and Sterling rolled down his window. "He caught up, huh?"

Brooks nodded. "Grabbed the ice-cream bar right off the roof."

"What did he do with it?" Diane asked.

"What do you think he did with it?" Brooks pointed at a dark shape along the shoulder of the road. Wayne switched on the van's brights. Suddenly the huge ice-cream bar was illuminated—with a huge bite taken out of it.

"At least he had the sense not to eat the whole thing," Diane said with a sigh.

On the darkened helipad near the Nevada State Militia airstrip, Charles Hendrickson leaned against the helicopter and puffed on a cigarette. Precious time was being lost waiting for final clearance. Through the window of the hut across the tarmac he could see Captain Meyerson sipping a mug of coffee and chatting with some of his ground crew.

Hendrickson dropped the butt of the cigarette to the ground and angrily mashed it out with his foot. Darn! If Wheeler was supposed to have such good connections in this state, why was it taking so long to get the final clearance for takeoff?

As if someone had heard him, a phone rang in the hut. Through the window, Hendrickson watched a man pick up the receiver and hand it to Meyerson. He watched Meyerson listen and nod, then hang up, finish his coffee, and pick up his helmet. A moment later the captain strolled out of the hut.

"You got final clearance, sir," he said.

"Good," Hendrickson said. "Let's move it."

Meyerson seemed to be in no hurry, but soon they were strapped into the helicopter and lifting off to the loud whir of the rotors. Hendrickson positioned himself behind the tranquilizer cannon in the cargo bay and pulled on a green flying helmet with a mike that put him in communication with Meyerson up front. As the helicopter rose into the air, he watched the blue streams of light along the airstrip grow smaller beneath them.

"Where to, sir?" Meyerson asked through his headset.

"Las Vegas," Hendrickson replied curtly.

The helicopter tilted to the right and began flying toward the distant lights of Las Vegas at what seemed to Hendrickson to be a leisurely pace.

"Can't you make this thing go any faster?" he asked impatiently. "That kid might be growing again!"

"This is as fast as we can safely go," Meyerson replied.

They stood beside the van, staring at the giant ice-cream bar with the bite taken out of it.

"Well, that didn't work," Sterling said. "What are we going to do now?"

Wayne shrugged. Brooks stared down at his feet. Only Diane still had a determined look.

"We need to get Adam to hold still," she insisted.

"In other words," Wayne said, "we need a miracle—a *big* miracle."

Diane stared at him, an idea starting to percolate in her mind—an incredible idea, but an idea nonetheless. "Wayne?"

"Yes?" Her husband looked up.

"Do you remember how we finally got Adam to be still long enough to have his picture taken?"

"You had to sit and hold him," Wayne said.

"That's right." Diane gently pulled her husband to the side and spoke quietly. "Adam needs me to tell him what he can and can't do, what he can and can't touch, and what's going to hurt him. I'm his mommy, Wayne. The problem is, to Adam his mommy is somebody very much bigger than he is."

As she said this last part, she turned and nodded slowly at the machine in the van. Wayne suddenly realized what she was implying.

"No!" he shook his head. "No way. It's crazy."

Diane put her hands on her husband's shoulders and looked straight into his eyes. "Wayne, for almost twenty years I've watched you have one crazy idea after another. Now it's time for me to have just one of my own."

Wayne gazed back into his wife's eyes. He knew that what she was proposing might mean losing her forever. Under any other circumstances, he would have refused absolutely. But he also knew why she wanted to do it: Because she loved her son. And because there seemed to be no other way to save him.

"All right," he nodded reluctantly. Diane threw

her arms around him and hugged, but Wayne pulled back. "There's just one problem."

"What?"

Wayne pointed at the Szalinski I in the back of the van. "The van's batteries must be pretty low. I doubt they can supply adequate power at this point."

"What are you two cooking up now?" Clifford Sterling asked as he joined them.

Diane and Wayne exchanged a glance and then told him. Sterling looked shocked at first but then nodded.

"It might be our only chance," he said.

"But we don't have the juice," Wayne added.

Sterling rubbed his eyes and glanced back at the small convoy. His eyes settled on the spotlight truck, and a smile creased his lips. "Oh, yes we do."

A few minutes later Sterling stood beside the generator truck reading gauges as the machine revved and whined. Two heavy electrical cables ran from the generator to the van.

"Preheating the lasers, Wayne," he called out. "Six hundred volts!"

While Diane watched expectantly, Wayne jammed the bottom of a broken soda bottle into the machine's filter pack. Everything was ready, but Wayne decided to take one last stab at changing Diane's mind.

"Diane," he said, "I should be doing this, not you."

"No, hon," Diane replied. "There's one thing every little kid knows: Daddies mean fun; mommies mean business."

"But you don't realize the chances you're taking," Wayne said desperately. "This thing was never meant to do anything like this. Too little power and you'll grow too slowly, like Adam. Too much power and—"

Before he could finish, Diane gently cradled his face in her hands. "I trust you, Wayne Szalinski. Heaven help me, but I do. Besides, you're the smartest guy I know."

"Which says a lot about—" Wayne started to say, but before he could finish the self-deprecating joke, his wife kissed him.

Suddenly the sound of a helicopter broke the night silence. They looked upward.

"TV crew?" Wayne asked.

Sterling looked through the binoculars and shook his head. "It's from the Nevada State Militia."

"Why them?" Diane asked.

"I'm not sure," Sterling said. "I do know that one of the board members has close ties with them. A man named Wheeler . . ." He paused as if realizing something, then looked knowingly at Wayne. ". . . a man who happens to be Charles Hendrickson's staunchest supporter."

Diane looked up at the helicopter, and Wayne saw her eyes narrow. "Wayne, it's time to get large."

* * *

Not far away Adam wandered along looking for something new to play with. Nick and Mandy had climbed out of the sports car and back to the top edge of the pocket again. In the distance they could hear the strains of rock music and saw a giant neon guitar sign with flashing strings.

"What's that?" Nick asked.

"The Hard Rock Cafe," Mandy said. "Judging from the direction we're going, I take it your brother likes to rock."

"I think he just likes to mangle guitars," Nick said.

Within a few moments, Adam had arrived outside the nightclub. The patrons inside must have heard him coming because they were streaming out of the place, screaming hysterically. But Adam had no interest in the nightclub. He just wanted the giant neon guitar.

As his brother reached for the guitar, Nick realized how much electricity it must have taken for it to be lit so brightly. Adam could electrocute himself!

"You better not touch that guitar!" he shouted.

"Big ow-eee, Adam!" Mandy screamed. "Don't touch!"

Adam did not choose this moment to start listening. The next thing they knew, he had ripped the guitar right off the building. The long electrical cables remained attached, and the guitar continued to glow in Adam's hands.

In a flash they were both shouting. "Put it down, Adam! Put the guitar down!"

Now another noise added to the confusion—the distant sound of a helicopter. Adam turned around and grinned with delight. "Air-pane!"

"Doesn't your brother know the difference between an airplane and a helicopter?" Mandy asked.

"Did you when you were two?" Nick asked back.

Mandy shrugged. "You've got a point."

"Air-pane!" Adam said again.

"Yes, Adam!" Nick shouted. "Airplane! Put the guitar down and go look at the airplane!"

In the air, several hundred yards away, Hendrickson readied the tranquilizer gun.

"I thought this was only a last resort, sir," Meyerson said through his headset.

"I don't see any other choice," Hendrickson said coldly. "Bring me into range and hold her steady."

"But sir!"

"Did you receive orders?" Hendrickson snapped irritably.

"Yes, sir."

"Then do what I tell you."

"I will, sir," Meyerson said. "It's just that if we hit him and he stumbles, he could fall into the crowd."

"We'll just have to hope he doesn't," Hendrickson replied coldly.

Captain Meyerson had heard enough. A few hundred yards away, the big kid was grinning and waving at them. As far as the helicopter pilot was concerned, that kid was about as big a threat to people as a hot air balloon. In the cargo bay he could see Hendrickson get the kid in the sights of the tranquilizer gun and start to squeeze the trigger. Just as the gun was about to fire, Meyerson jerked the helicopter's control stick, causing the aircraft to lurch sideways.

The gun went off, and the tranquilizer bullet hit the neon guitar with a *bang!* A shower of sparks flew up in front of Adam's eyes, followed by a great cloud of white smoke.

"AHHH!" Frightened by the attack, Adam let go of the guitar, and it crashed to the ground.

"They're shooting at Adam!" Nick shouted.

"Hey, phlegm wad!" Mandy shook her fist at the helicopter. "Pick on someone your own size!"

"WHHHAAA!" Frightened by the explosion, Adam started rubbing his eyes and crying.

"Hold on!" Nick shouted as the boy's chest heaved in and out with sobs.

"No air pane!" Adam wailed as the helicopter circled around him.

Inside, Hendrickson patiently reloaded the tranquilizer gun. "I assume that little maneuver was an error, Captain," he said through gritted teeth. "Now pull her around again and this time hold her steady or I'll have you busted down to latrine mopper."

Meyerson reluctantly brought the helicopter around. Once again Hendrickson took aim with the tranquilizer cannon. Slowly, his finger closed around the trigger. . . .

A huge shadow suddenly fell over the helicopter.

In his ten years of flying, Captain Meyerson had never felt a chopper behave like this. Why, it was as though a giant hand had reached up and grabbed it!

And that, in fact, was precisely what had happened. The next thing they knew, the chopper was nose to nose with a very angry-looking Diane. Hendrickson froze with fear as Diane glared into the cargo bay at him.

"Back off!" she ordered.

Hendrickson's hands came off the tranquilizer gun, and Meyerson let go of the helicopter's controls.

"Yes, ma'am," he said with a smile.

Not far away, Nick and Mandy had watched Diane, now even larger than Adam, pluck the helicopter out of the sky and shout at it.

"Is that your mother?" Mandy asked.

"Yeah."

Mandy shook her head. "Weird family."

They watched as Diane put the helicopter on the ground and held her huge arms out toward Adam. "Come here, baby."

"Mama!" Adam cried. As he bounded toward her, Nick and Mandy lost their grip on the edge of the pocket and fell back inside.

"Everything's going to be okay." Diane began to cry as she finally got her son back into her arms again. "Mommy's here now."

"Mama cwy-ing?" Adam asked quizzically.

"Yes, dear," Diane sniffed. "Mommy's crying. It's okay to cry when you're so happy."

She picked him up and hugged him to her. Inside Adam's pocket, Nick and Mandy were almost crushed.

"Hey, Mom!" Nick shouted. "Take it easy, okay?"

But his voice was muffled in the clothing, so Diane didn't hear him as she turned Adam around and gestured at the caravan of tiny trucks on the ground below.

"Look at Daddy, Adam," she said.

"Da-da?" Adam looked around, puzzled.

"Down there." She pointed down at the tiny humans working frantically around the van and the generator truck.

"Give it everything it's got!" Wayne was shouting as he aimed the Szalinski I up at his enormous wife and child.

"We better do it!" Sterling shouted back as he wiped the sweat off his brow. "The bearings on the generator are going to burn out any second!"

"What's the voltage reading?" Wayne shouted.

"Fourteen-fifty," Sterling answered. "Do it, Wayne! It's all she's got!"

"Now hold still just like we're having our picture taken," Diane told her son. "Say cheese, Adam."

"Cheese," Adam said.

Ka-blam!

There was a huge explosion. Wayne felt himself become airborne, flying backward. He landed on

215

his back, but nothing felt broken and he quickly got up. For a moment all he could see was smoke. His face felt scorched, and he could smell singed hair. The generator must've blown! But did the machine have time to work? Wayne waved his arms frantically, trying to clear the smoke. There were no huge people in sight. Where were they?

As the smoke cleared, Wayne saw Adam standing in the middle of the road. He rushed toward him, scooping him up in his arms and hugging him.

"Oh, Adam!" he laughed.

Sterling came out of the smoke, covered with black soot but with a smile on his face. "You gave us quite a scare, little man." He rubbed Adam affectionately on the head.

Diane staggered up, still dazzled from the sudden change of size. She hugged Wayne and Adam and whispered in her husband's ear. "I knew you could do it."

Wayne hugged her back. He knew that she really meant it. She believed in him, and after getting Adam back, that was the next best feeling in the world.

"Well, Szalinski, you pulled it off," a voice suddenly interrupted them. "Who would have thought?"

The happy little group broke apart as Hendrickson strolled up, acting as if nothing had happened. Before Wayne could answer him, Diane stepped forward, holding Adam on her hip.

"Oh, Dr. Hendrickson," she said with a smile,

"when you were in the helicopter, it looked like you were aiming some sort of gun at my baby."

"Just loaded with tranquilizer cartridges," Hendrickson replied. "They wouldn't have hurt him, I assure you."

"I see," Diane said as she turned to her husband. "Wayne, dear, would you take Adam for a second?"

Wayne took the baby. Diane turned around, pulled back her fist and . . . *smash!* She decked Hendrickson with a blow to the jaw.

"Let that be a lesson," Wayne told Adam. "Never cross Mommy."

Sterling stood over the unconscious man and called to the emergency services personnel. "Could we have some help over here? Dr. Hendrickson has been overcome with excitement at the prospect of finding a new career."

Once again the Szalinskis hugged each other. Then Diane realized that Nick and Mandy weren't there.

"Wayne," she gasped. "The kids! Nick and Mandy!"

"Weren't they . . . ?" Wayne was struck by the realization. ". . . . in Adam's pocket?"

Diane quickly bent down and searched Adam's pocket. There was nothing but a hole at the bottom. "Oh no!" she cried. "Don't tell me!"

"Honey!" Wayne gasped. "I shrunk the kids!" He looked at the startled faces around them. "Nobody move!"

"How are you going to find them?" Sterling asked.

"Don't worry, I have highly specialized equipment for dealing with this," Wayne said hurriedly and turned to his wife. "Honey, in the van. I'll need my magnifying helmet and the dog."

Nick and Mandy sat in the sports car and watched the eastern sky turn light as dawn approached. They were parked at the edge of the desert with the top down. Mandy seemed comfortable and obviously relieved that they were no longer prisoners in Adam's pocket. Nick was certain she thought they were still normal size. Fortunately it was still relatively dark, and she hadn't noticed the seemingly huge cigarette butt lying on the ground behind them.

Nick turned on the car's radio, and they caught part of an early morning newscast:

> The Szalinski Two is the brainchild of inventor Wayne Szalinski. Though the existence of such a size- and mass-altering device has been rumored for years, the events in Las Vegas tonight certainly confirm it. There are those who are speculating

that inventor Szalinski may be in line for a Nobel Prize. Others indicate that this may be the invention of the century. Famed American industrialist Clifford Sterling has also said that Szalinski may be stepping into his position as head of Sterling Labs. . . .

Mandy reached over and turned the radio off, then stayed close, leaning against Nick's shoulder.

"I guess your father's about the most famous guy in the world tonight," she said.

Nick couldn't help but smile. "I guess."

"And I guess you're the bravest," Mandy added, kissing him on the cheek. "Thanks for saving my life."

Nick sort of stretched and let his arm fall over the back of Mandy's seat. "Oh, it wasn't much," he said, then caught himself. "I didn't mean your life wasn't much. I mean, what I did wasn't so much."

"I know what you meant." Mandy snuggled next to him. "So, how long do you think it will take before they find us?"

"Oh, I don't know." Nick happened to glance in the rearview mirror and stopped. In the mirror he could see a huge eye enlarged by a magnifying glass. Nick knew it was his father. He turned slightly behind him and spoke a little louder. "I think it might be a while before they find us."

Towering behind them, Wayne knew just who his son was addressing with those last words. He sat back on the roadside and held Quark at bay while he removed the magnifying helmet.

Meanwhile, still unaware that they had company, Mandy looked up at Nick. "You know, you're kind of different, Nick. Like your dad."

"Oh, we're not that different," Nick said.

"Believe me, you are," Mandy insisted, taking his arm from behind the seat and draping it over her shoulders. "But I think that's nice. Maybe the world needs people who are different. Like, they look at things differently, you know?"

Nick just smiled. With his arm around her shoulders he was ready to agree with just about anything she said.

Wayne sensed someone behind him. It was Diane, carrying Adam.

"Did you find them?" she asked.

"Yeah." Wayne got to his feet. "But let's give them some time, okay?"

"Why?" Diane asked. "What's going on?"

Wayne didn't answer. He just winked at Adam, who stared down at the two tiny figures in the tiny yellow car. When he saw what they were doing, he covered his eyes with his hands for a moment, then held his nose and stuck out his tongue.

Diane and Wayne chuckled quietly. It was great to have their son back to normal.

About the Author

Todd Strasser has written many award-winning novels for young and teenage readers, including *The Diving Bell, Beyond the Reef, The Accident,* and *Friends till the End.* He is a frequent speaker at schools and conferences. He and his wife have two normal-sized children and live in a suburb of New York City.